Welcome

Gone to the

Jina

Shh!! Studying—
please do not disturb!

Mary Beth

GO AWAY!!!

Andie

Hey, guys!
Meet me downstairs in the common room. Bring popcorn!

Lauren

Join Andie, Jina, Mary Beth, and Lauren for more fun at the Riding Academy!

#1 • *A Horse for Mary Beth*
#2 • *Andie Out of Control*
#3 • *Jina Rides to Win*
#4 • *Lessons for Lauren*
#5 • *Mary Beth's Haunted Ride*
#6 • *Andie Shows Off*
#7 • *Jina's Pain-in-the-Neck Pony*

And coming soon:

#8 • *The Craziest Horse Show Ever*
#9 • *Andie's Risky Business*

"It's just you and me, buddy," Jina told Applejacks. "We're making friends, right?"

With one hand on the lead rope, Jina reached around the doorway for her saddle and pad. Carefully, she set them on the pony's back, then smoothed the pad under the saddle.

She walked around Applejacks' head to his other side and made sure the girth was straight. When she walked back, she scratched his forehead. He wiggled his upper lip happily.

So far, so good.

But when she reached for the girth, Applejacks turned and stared at her. His ears flattened against his head. Then he shook his head, his mane flying, as if to say no.

Butterflies churned in Jina's stomach. Grabbing the end of the girth, she slid the straps through the buckles. Suddenly, without warning, Applejacks snaked his head around.

His mouth wide open, the pony sunk his teeth into Jina's wrist!

Jina's Pain-in-the-Neck Pony

by Alison Hart

BULLSEYE BOOKS
Random House New York

A BULLSEYE BOOK PUBLISHED BY RANDOM HOUSE, INC.

 Published in the United States by Random House, Inc., New York, and simultaneously in Canada by Random House of Canada Limited, Toronto.

Library of Congress Catalog Card Number: 94-67692

ISBN: 0-679-87119-5

RL: 4.9

Manufactured in the United States of America

10 9 8 7 6 5 4 3 2 1

"Oh, Ji-i-ina!" a sweet voice called into the bathroom of suite 4B. "Since you're already in there, how about getting me a drink of water?"

Jina Williams rolled her golden eyes, then spit toothpaste into the sink.

Do this, do that. Get me this, get me that. It was all she'd heard from Andie since her roommate had hurt her knee and was stuck in bed. And it was starting to drive her crazy.

"Jina? Did you hear me?" Andie's voice didn't sound so sweet this time.

"I heard you," Jina called back, "but I'm brushing my teeth. When I'm finished, I'll bring you your drink.

"And dump it over your head," she added under her breath. Instantly, she regretted her words. Andie's knee really was hurting her, and she was super-upset because her father wouldn't buy Mr. Magic, the horse Andie was in love with. Besides, Andie only had to stay in bed for one more day. Jina knew she would just have to put up with it until then.

"Jina-a-a! What are you *doing* in there? I'm dying of thirst."

Jina made a face in the mirror. She *hoped* she could stand it one more day. At least this afternoon she could escape to Middlefield Stables. Then her other two roommates, Lauren Remick and Mary Beth Finney, would get to be Andie's slaves. Jina rinsed her mouth and stuck her toothbrush and toothpaste back into her shower bucket.

Usually she enjoyed her private riding lessons at Middlefield with her trainer, Todd Jenkins. But today she would have to ride Applejacks again.

And she wasn't looking forward to that at all.

"I said, what's going on in here?"

Jina spun around. Andie was standing in the doorway of the bathroom, dressed in baggy sweats. Her sore knee was cocked as she leaned her weight against the doorjamb.

"What are you doing out of bed?" Jina asked sharply.

Andie frowned impatiently. Her usually unruly hair was plastered against her head from lying on a pillow for two days. "I'm getting my *own* drink. I thought you'd fallen in the toilet or something."

Jina took Andie's elbow and steered her back to bed. The four sixth-grade roommates shared a suite at Foxhall Academy, a private girls' boarding school in Maryland.

On the first day of school, Andie had claimed the bed by the window. Now her rumpled blanket and pillow were strewn with half-eaten cookies.

Jina wrinkled her nose at the mess. "Disgusting."

"They sure were." Andie snorted as she balanced carefully on one foot. "Mary Beth bought me those cheapo chocolate chips from the snack bar."

"I meant your *bed*," Jina said, briskly brushing off Andie's blanket. Crumbs flew everywhere. "Mrs. Shiroo's going to throw a fit." The dorm mother often held surprise inspections.

Andie nodded as she sat on the edge of the bed. "Yeah. It would be a good idea if you swept the floor. But before you do, get me that glass of water, okay?"

Jina gave a mock "Yes, Your Majesty."

"And don't forget breakfast," Andie added. "I've got my order right here—somewhere."

Andie reached over and began to rummage through the junk on her bed stand. The top was jammed with books, half-torn magazines, and sticky candy wrappers. Finally, she pulled a piece of paper from under a drinking glass filled with murky liquid.

Jina grimaced as she took a corner of the paper between two fingers. "It's all wet."

"Oh, I spilled some soda on it, but you can still read what I want." Andie swung her legs onto the bed and leaned back against her pillows. "Ahh. This is the life. Maids to wait on me. No classes all day."

"You'll still have to make up the work," Jina reminded her. She folded the soggy list and stuck it in her pocket, then walked over to the wardrobe that all the girls shared.

"At least you won't miss riding. It's canceled today because of the rain."

"*And* because old Caufield needs a day off

after Parents' Weekend." Andie chuckled. "It was a little wild."

"*You* were wild," Jina said as she pulled on her coat. To impress her father, Andie had jumped Magic before the horse was ready and had gotten thrown.

Andie groaned. "Don't remind me. I can't believe I have to wait a whole week before I can ride Magic again. Mrs. Caufield said I *might* be able to take him to the interschool show in two weeks. They'll have a walk-trot class." Andie scowled. "Me in a baby class. I'll be competing against dopey beginning riders like Mary Beth."

Their roommate Mary Beth was just learning to ride, and Andie never let her forget it.

"Give it a break, Andie." Jina sighed. It had been over a month since she'd ridden her horse, Superstar. At their last show, he'd bowed a tendon. "At least you'll get to compete. I won't be able to ride Superstar at all."

"Maybe you can take Rotten Apple to the show," Andie said grinning.

"*Applejacks*," Jina corrected her roommate, even though Andie's name for the pony was probably closer to the truth.

With another sigh, Jina buttoned her raincoat and headed for the door. She knew she had to hurry if she was going to bring back a ton of breakfast for Andie.

"See you," she called over her shoulder as she opened the door.

"And don't forget, *blueberry* muffins—with lots of butter," Andie called after her.

Jina hurried down the hall. The usually bustling dorm was quiet and empty. Jina was one of the few students who didn't have an eight o'clock class. Her schedule had been set up so she'd have extra time to study in the morning. When she'd first come to Foxhall, preparing for shows with Superstar had taken most of her time and energy later in the day.

Jina reached the first floor of Bracken Hall and pushed open the heavy exit door. Gray clouds darkened the sky, and a cold rain beat on the sidewalks. She shoved her hands in her pockets and quickly cut across the grassy courtyard to the cafeteria.

"Jina!" Lauren waved from the steps of Eaton Hall. She and Mary Beth were huddled under a Cinderella umbrella. Lauren's blond head came only to Mary Beth's shoulder.

Mary Beth was munching a bagel smeared with cream cheese. Her reddish-brown bangs, plastered on her forehead, were damp from the rain.

Jina pulled her hood tighter around her head and broke into a jog. Rain splattered her cheeks and splashed on her pant legs.

"Hi, guys," she greeted her two roommates as she leaped up the steps and ducked under the overhang. "Did you finish breakfast already?"

Lauren nodded. "Our first class starts in five minutes. Lucky *you,* getting to sleep late."

"You mean getting to listen to Sergeant Perez," Jina said. "She even gave me her breakfast order." Whipping the crumpled list from the pocket of her raincoat she read, "Two eggs, one box of Frosted Flakes, two blueberry muffins..."

Mary Beth rolled her eyes.

"How much longer does Her Highness have to stay in bed?"

"Until tomorrow," Lauren replied. Suddenly, her blue eyes widened in horror. "Oh, no! That means we'll have to listen to her all afternoon!"

Mary Beth gulped hard. "You're right. Riding's been canceled because of the rain."

Lauren grabbed Jina's wrist. "Jina, you've

got to let Mary Beth and me go with you to Middlefield this afternoon."

"Oh, come on, guys," Jina said glancing back and forth at her roommates. "Andie's not *that* bad."

"Oh, yes, she is," Lauren declared. "And we'll be cooped up in the suite with her all afternoon. She'll drive us crazy!"

Mary Beth leaned closer to Jina.

"Do you want to see us crazier than we already are?"

"Uh, no, but—" Jina racked her brain for a reason why her roommates shouldn't go with her to Middlefield "—you probably couldn't get permission."

"Sure we can!" Lauren said. "Mrs. Volkert let me go with you before."

Mary Beth nodded. "Besides, we're dying to see you ride Applejacks. He's so-o-o cute and sweet."

Cute and sweet! Jina groaned silently. *If only they knew.*

"Ple-ease," Lauren said.

Jina shook her head. Mary Beth and Lauren seemed determined to go with her. How could she tell them she didn't want them to come?

"Well, I—" Jina stammered. Rain dripped off the hem of her coat. "I—"

She bit her lip. Why didn't she just tell her roommates the real reason she didn't want them coming to watch her ride?

"You don't want us to go to Middlefield with you, do you?" Mary Beth demanded, breaking into Jina's thoughts.

Jina focused her attention back on her roommates. Lauren and Mary Beth were looking at her curiously.

"Does it have something to do with Todd?" Lauren asked. "Do you like him, too?"

Jina shook her head. "Come on, Lauren. That's a dumb idea." Lauren had had a crush on Todd ever since she'd met him. "He's my trainer. Besides, he's way too old."

"Okay, then." Mary Beth put her hands on her hips. "Why don't you want us to come?"

Jina's shoulders sagged. Her roommates weren't going to quit bugging her until she told them the truth.

"Because I don't want you to watch me ride Applejacks," she said finally.

Lauren and Mary Beth exchanged puzzled glances. "Why not?" they chorused.

"Because every time I ride that stupid pony, he tries to buck me off. And today he just might do it."

Mary Beth's brows shot up in surprise. "Buck *you* off? No way! You're the best rider at Foxhall."

"I don't believe you, either," Lauren scoffed. "Besides, Applejacks is so sweet."

"Believe it." Jina abruptly turned and reached for the handle of the cafeteria door. At the same time, two older girls pushed open the door from the inside, almost knocking her off the steps.

Jina grabbed the wrought-iron railing and steadied herself. Lauren and Mary Beth backed out of the way.

Jina recognized the two girls. The blonde was Ashley Stewart, a junior who had been Lauren's math tutor. She was bundled up in a long wool cape and a velour scarf. The brunette was Ashley's roommate, Penny. She was dressed in a green army fatigue coat and combat boots.

"Well, excu-u-use me," Penny said sarcastically. "If I'd known it was just a bunch of sixth-graders, I would have pushed a little harder."

Penny giggled, then narrowed her eyes at Lauren. "Hey, Ash," she said, nudging the blond girl with her elbow, "isn't that the little worm who sicced the doctors on you?"

Ashley nodded. Her face was pale under her striped hood. By now, everyone at Foxhall knew she was battling an eating disorder. She brushed rudely past Jina and her roommates. "Come on, Pen, we have to get to class."

Jina glanced at Lauren. Her roommate was clutching the umbrella handle tightly, and Jina saw her face crumple as Penny threw her a disdainful look on her way down the stairs. Jina felt sorry for Lauren. Still, she was glad Ashley hadn't said something nasty to *her,* like, "Hey, Williams, how's your rich, famous mom?"

Before Superstar's accident, she and Ashley had been intense rivals. Ashley never let her forget that many of the Foxhall students saw her only as talk show host Myra Golden's daughter.

But when Ashley reached the bottom step, she turned and looked back at Jina. "So, Williams, I hear you're going to ride that Middlefield pony at some of the indoor shows this winter." The older girl's gaze was intense under the hood of her cape.

"Uh, yeah, I am," Jina answered hesitantly. *What was Ashley was getting at?*

A ghost of a smile flickered across Ashley's lips. "Then we just may be competing against each other again."

Jina's heart skipped a beat. "What do you mean?" she asked.

"Well, it's pretty certain I'm going to win the Horse of the Year Award, so I've had plenty of offers from people who want me to ride their horses *and* ponies," Ashley said. She gave Jina a confident smile. "I'll see you at the shows."

Jina swallowed hard. "Yeah, see you," she croaked as Ashley and Penny sauntered across the courtyard. A cold gust of wind blew a spray of rain in her face, making her shiver.

"Well, she sure hasn't gotten any nicer," Mary Beth said, turning to Lauren. "I thought Ashley had decided to forgive you for telling that doctor about all that crazy dieting she was doing."

Lauren just shrugged, but Jina could tell by her roommate's expression that she was still upset over the whole thing with Ashley. For a while, Lauren had practically worshiped the older girl.

"My sister says Ashley doesn't hate me anymore, but I don't think we'll ever be friends again," Lauren said, "and it looks like Ashley's got it in for you again, too, Jina. She's supercompetitive."

"I'm not going to worry about it," Jina said, even though she already was. "Besides, Applejacks and I won't be going to any shows real soon."

Maybe never, she added silently. That pony was impossible.

"Hah!" Mary Beth grinned at Lauren. "I bet she's just exaggerating about Applejacks. She's taking him to the interschool show."

Lauren gave Jina a sideways glance.

"Yeah, she's too good a rider to let some pony get the better of her. But we'll find out the truth when we watch her this afternoon, right, roomies?"

Jina smiled resignedly. "Right."

"This place is so-o-o-o cool," Mary Beth exclaimed later that afternoon. She was standing next to Jina in the wide, spotless aisle of the barn at Middlefield Stables. Even though it was still rainy and cold outside, the huge building was climate controlled, so it was light, airy and warm. "I feel like I died and went to horse heaven."

"Hey, guys. Come over here!" Lauren called, waving excitedly. She was standing in front of a steel-mesh screen stall door.

Slowly, Jina followed Mary Beth, who was already rushing toward Lauren. Ever since the Foxhall van had dropped them off at Middlefield, Jina's stomach had been twisting and churning. She couldn't stop thinking about what Applejacks might do today—and how ridiculous she'd look in front of her roommates.

"What is it?" Mary Beth peered inside the stall. A huge, chestnut horse came over and snuffled at the screen. With a squeak, Mary Beth jerked back.

Lauren stuck one finger through the mesh, cooing and stroking the horse's nose.

"I can't believe it," she whispered, sounding awestruck. "I'm actually patting *Jazz Man*."

"Jazz Man?" Mary Beth repeated in a puzzled voice. "Who's that?"

"The horse that won the Volvo World Cup

Finals, dummy! See? His name's on his halter," Lauren said. "Didn't you see that article about him in *HorsePlay* magazine?" Twisting around, she looked pointedly at Jina. "You didn't tell me he was stabled here."

Jina shrugged. Her mind was hardly on Jazz Man right now. "Sorry, I guess I forgot. Listen, guys," she added quickly, "I've got to go find Todd."

With a wave to her roommates, Jina strode down the aisle to the tack room. When she reached the door, she opened it and peered in. The smell of saddle soap and leather filled her lungs.

One paneled wall of the spacious room was lined with bridles and another with saddles. A third was covered with ribbons. A shelf built about a foot below the ceiling ran all around the room, gleaming with plaques and trophies.

The office door was open. Jina could see the edge of the desk and the swivel chair. Todd was nowhere in sight.

She left the tack room and made her way down the aisle. A few of the working students were grooming horses and mucking stalls. They were older than Jina—most of them high school or college-age kids who worked at the stable in return for lessons.

Jina waved to Spencer, Todd's younger brother. He was brushing a big bay horse standing in crossties. From a distance, Jina had thought Spencer was Todd. The two of them looked a lot alike.

Jina stopped for a while to watch the students work. They always seemed to be having so much fun. In a way, she envied them. She wondered what it would be like not having a mother who could buy her anything she wanted.

Jina moved on, cutting through the concrete washroom to the other side of the barn. A few moments later, she walked into a room filled with chairs. The wall opposite the door had a huge Plexiglas window that overlooked the indoor arena.

Todd was in the middle of the arena longing Applejacks. The gray pony trotted steadily around him in a circle. Whitney Chambers, Apple's young owner, was perched in the saddle. Whitney posted energetically, a huge grin on her face. Several blond curls that had escaped from under her helmet bounced against her cheek.

"Jina!" she heard Lauren call from the aisle.

Jina didn't answer. She couldn't tear her eyes away from Applejacks.

Even though he was only fourteen hands, eight inches smaller than Superstar, the pony had a long stride—like a miniature Thoroughbred. His ears were pricked forward eagerly, and his neck arched prettily as he trotted around the circle.

He was as calm and quiet as one of Foxhall's old school horses.

I don't believe it, Jina thought, slumping into one of the chairs facing the window. *Applejacks really is cute and sweet. I must have been crazy to think he was a problem horse.*

She let out her breath, and the knot in her stomach started to unwind. All her worrying had been for nothing.

Everything was going to be okay.

"Look, there's Whitney and Applejacks!"

Lauren's excited squeal made Jina jump in her chair. Her two roommates were standing behind her, staring out the observation window.

Just then, Applejacks halted, and Todd walked over to talk to Whitney. The young trainer was well built but slender with golden-blond hair that curled on his collar. He wore faded jeans, barn boots, and a down vest over a black turtleneck.

"He is so-o-o-o cute," Mary Beth exclaimed for the tenth time. Jina rolled her eyes.

Lauren sighed. "I have to keep reminding myself he's too old for me."

Mary Beth shot her a puzzled look. "I was talking about Applejacks."

Lauren blushed; even Jina had to giggle.

"Applejacks is cute, too," Lauren said quickly. "And what a great mover for such a little pony!" She slid into the chair beside Jina's. "You're so lucky you get to ride him."

"Yeah, I am," Jina said. For once she felt as if she meant it.

Todd said something to Whitney, then pointed toward the window. Twisting around in the saddle, Whitney waved to the girls excitedly.

"Whitney's a cutie, too," Lauren said. "Just look at that neat outfit she's wearing. Schooling sweats just her size. I wish I had a little sister. Especially one who liked to ride."

Jina stood up. "I guess Todd's ready for me. I'd better get my saddle."

"We'll watch from here," Mary Beth said. "That way we'll stay nice and warm."

"Good luck!" Lauren called as Jina left the room.

"Thanks," Jina called back. She hoped she wouldn't need it. *Think positive,* she reminded herself.

Jina found her riding helmet and her saddle where she'd left them—propped against a wall in the tack room. It was her older saddle, the one she used for schooling.

She stuck her helmet on her head and fastened the strap. Then she picked the saddle up by the pommel and cantle, rearranged the girth so it wouldn't drag, and went to find Todd. He was leading Applejacks to the entrance of the arena.

"Jina!" Whitney said happily when she saw her coming. The little girl slid off the pony, landing in the tanbark. Whirling around, she hugged Jina's side. "I'm so glad to see you! Are you riding Apple today? He was so good. I just love him!"

Raising her arms high, the little girl fell against Applejacks's neck. The pony didn't budge. She kissed him noisily, then gave Jina a huge smile. "And I love you!" she said.

Jina had to laugh. She'd never seen a kid with so much energy.

"Whitney." Todd's voice was firm. "You need to take off your saddle so Jina can put hers on."

Whitney ignored him. "Was that Lauren and Mary Beth I saw?" she asked. "Did they come with you?"

Jina nodded. "They're still in the observation room."

"Yippee!" Whitney jumped up and down. "I'm going to say hi to them." Unsnapping her helmet, she raced through the wide doorway.

"Whitney!" Todd called after her. "Your saddle!"

But the little girl was already gone.

Todd groaned in exasperation.

"She's just excited. I'll take the saddle off," Jina offered.

"No, I've got it." As Todd unbuckled the girth, he glanced sideways at Jina. "Think you're ready to ride Apple today?"

She nodded firmly. "Yes."

"I worked with him and Whitney this weekend, and he's been doing well," Todd said. "Let's hope that bucking business is over with."

"I can handle it," Jina said confidently.

Todd slid off Whitney's saddle and pad and hung them over the gate that separated the indoor arena from the main barn. Applejacks turned his head to look at Jina. His brown eyes were calm but curious.

"Hi, Apple," Jina greeted him.

Todd took Jina's saddle and pad from her and set them on the gray's back. Instantly, the pony pinned his ears, giving them both a nasty look.

"Ignore him," Todd said.

"Doesn't he like being tacked up?" Jina asked, hoping that was all that was wrong.

Todd didn't answer right away. He smoothed the saddle pad, then bent over and reached under the pony's belly to grab the girth dangling on the other side.

"He's usually fine. You have to remember he's still green. But he's got to get used to everything if Whitney's going to handle him."

Todd pulled the girth up several holes. Applejacks swished his tail and kicked out with his left hoof. Jina jumped backward.

Todd kneed the pony in the stomach. "Knock it off," he scolded.

Jina pressed her lips together. Five minutes ago the pony had been dead quiet. What was wrong with him now? Was it her?

"Ready?" Todd turned to face her.

Jina hesitated, then said, "Sure!" But she knew she didn't sound so sure.

Todd led Applejacks out into the arena. Two

riders were schooling their horses at one end. Rain beat on the metal roof, echoing through the huge building.

Jina shivered as she followed Todd. It was cold in the arena. She wished she'd worn her chaps and a warmer jacket.

Todd halted Applejacks, checked the girth, and pulled down the stirrup irons. "Need a leg up?"

Jina shook her head. Standing by the pony's left shoulder, she gathered the reins. She stuck her left toe in the stirrup irons, hopped on her right foot, and mounted. Immediately, Applejacks hollowed his back and pinned his ears back. *Ignore him,* Jina told herself, remembering what Todd had said. Then a flurry of movement to her left caught her eye.

Mary Beth, Lauren, and Whitney were in the observation room, their noses pressed to the window. Whitney was standing on a chair between the two older girls. All three waved, and even though Jina couldn't hear them, she could tell they were giggling hysterically.

Were they laughing at her?

"Jina," Todd said sharply, "you're as bad as Whitney. Pay attention."

Jina snapped her head around. "Sorry."

Applejacks swung his hindquarters sideways and swished his tail.

"Look, Todd," Jina said. "Applejacks is already acting strange, and I'm just sitting on him. What do you want me to do?"

Todd furrowed his brow. "I don't know why he's giving you trouble. Go ahead and walk him in a circle around me. Keep a light rein, but use plenty of leg to make him pay attention. You've got to remember, he's not a made horse like Superstar. He's trying you out."

Jina nodded. Tightening the reins, she squeezed Applejacks into a walk. His back was still hollow, so his stride was short and choppy.

"Make small circles around me," Todd called. "Deep seat, lighten up on your rein, and use more leg to get him moving forward."

Jina followed Todd's instructions. Applejacks settled into a normal walk, but his pinned-back ears told Jina he was obeying reluctantly.

The trot wasn't any better. The pony's shorter, quicker strides made Jina tense. She wasn't sure why Applejacks felt so stiff beneath her. *Maybe I'm just not used to a pony trot*, she thought.

"Relax, Jina," Todd called. "No wonder he doesn't look happy. You're like a board."

Jina flushed under her helmet. She took a deep breath, trying to loosen her body.

Wistfully, she thought back to her last lesson at Middlefield on Superstar. It had been great. Superstar had been so willing and eager—

A sudden jolt threw Jina abruptly forward, and she caught herself on the pony's neck. He stopped dead.

"Jina!" Todd shouted. "Why did you let him stop like that? Is your brain turned off or what?"

Jina's cheeks burned. It had been a whole month since she'd taken a lesson with Todd, and his sharp tone stung.

"Sorry." She pressed her calves against the pony's side, asking him to walk. Applejacks pinned his ears back. He wouldn't budge. Turning, he bit at Jina's right boot.

Tears pricked Jina's eyes. She couldn't believe this was happening.

Todd strode toward her, his lips pressed together in a firm line. "What is going on?" he demanded. "Ten minutes ago, that pony was doing great. Then you get on him, and he starts acting up!"

Slowly Jina shook her head.

"I don't know what's wrong," she said, her voice quivering.

But she did know what was wrong.

Applejacks *hated* her!

Jina glanced back at the window overlooking the arena. Lauren, Mary Beth, and Whitney were waving and pointing and giggling.

Jina looked away quickly. Even though she couldn't hear the girls, she knew what they were saying.

Can you believe it? Jina can't ride Applejacks!

"Dig your heels in his sides and get him moving," Todd said. He was starting to sound impatient. "If I wasn't so big, I'd get on him myself."

Jina nodded, her fingers tensing on the reins. Applejacks hated her, Todd was mad, and her friends were probably talking about what a lousy rider she was.

What next?

She gave the pony a swift kick. He took two uneven steps, then moved into a hurried, bouncy trot. When they'd circled twice around Todd, the trainer told them to halt.

"Okay, Jina. Let's quit while we're ahead," Todd said. "Something's definitely wrong. I'll get one of my other students to try him tomorrow. Then you can ride him again Wednesday. Maybe by then, I will have figured out what's going on."

Jina's shoulders sagged with relief. At least Todd wasn't totally blaming it all on her. And for once Applejacks hadn't bucked. Maybe that was a good sign.

Quickly she dismounted before Applejacks tried something else. When she slid the reins over his head, the pony eyed her warily.

Jina eyed him back. She didn't know what she had done to that pony to deserve so many nasty looks.

Maybe I could come earlier on Wednesday, Jina thought. *I could groom him and feed him some horse treats. Then he might be better.*

Todd ran up the stirrups. Then he took the reins from Jina and started to lead Applejacks from the arena.

"Todd, wait." Jina hurried to keep up with him. "I think Applejacks just doesn't like me. Maybe I need to make friends with him."

Todd raised one brow. "What you need to do is *ride* him. He knows you're a little scared."

"I'm not scared," Jina said quickly.

"Sure." Todd chucked her on the arm. "Hey, don't take it so hard. I told you this would be a good experience, remember? You and Superstar were a perfect team. Now it's time to develop confidence on a not-so-perfect horse."

Jina smiled weakly.

"Maybe you're right," Todd added as they reached the barn aisle. "Making friends with Applejacks is a good idea." He unbuckled the pony's girth and slid off the saddle.

"Jina! Jina!" Whitney came racing around the corner. She crashed into Jina and threw her arms around her waist.

"Why did you quit riding Apple? Why didn't you canter? Why did he stop? Aren't you ever going to jump him?"

"Um," Jina stammered. Whitney clung to her and stared up at Jina with wide blue eyes.

"I told Jina to dismount," Todd said as he propped Jina's saddle against the wall. "Apple's had enough for today. You two girls need to cool him off and give him a good brushing."

He handed the reins to Jina. "Whitney, your mom should be here any minute. So get busy."

When Todd left, Whitney grabbed Jina's hand.

"Come on. I want to show you my new show bridle!" She tugged Jina toward the office.

"We have to finish untacking Apple first," Jina said, "and cool him off."

"No." Whitney stamped her foot. "I want to show you the bridle before my mother comes."

"Whitney—"

Just then, Lauren and Mary Beth came up.

"Hey, Jina, that was quite a show out there," Mary Beth said. "Applejacks was so slow and poky it reminded me of my lessons on Dan." She giggled. Jina said nothing. She knew Mary Beth wasn't trying to be mean. If Andie had made the same remark, it would have been different.

"I wonder why poor Applejacks was so balky," Lauren said, stroking the pony's nose. Taking the sides of his bridle in both hands, she lifted his head so it was even with her own. "Why were you giving my roommate such a hard time, you cutie-pie?" she asked him in a baby voice.

Whitney stamped her foot again. "*Now*, Jina!"

"Now what?" Mary Beth asked, looking from Whitney to Jina.

Jina sighed. "Whitney wants to show me Apple's new bridle before her mother comes. But we have to—"

"Well, you guys go ahead," Lauren interrupted. "Mary Beth and I can untack Applejacks and cool him off. Right, you little sweetie?" She kissed the pony again and rubbed his forehead.

"Thanks, Lauren, but Whitney and I are supposed to—" Jina began.

"Oh, no! My mom is here!" Whitney wailed.

Mrs. Chambers was stepping through the big sliding door at the end of the aisle. She wore high heels and a long camel-colored coat.

Whitney shot Jina an anguished look.

Jina gave in. "All right, show me the bridle."

"Goody." Whitney smiled again and started pulling Jina down the aisle. They reached the tack room door at the same time as Mrs. Chambers.

"Hello, Jina," Whitney's mother said

politely. Her blond hair was smoothed into a sleek French twist. She wore two glittery diamond earrings and perfect makeup.

"Hi, Mrs. Chambers," Jina said.

"How was your lesson, Whitney?" She leaned over to give her daughter a hug.

The little girl jerked away. "Fine." Turning from her mother, she darted into the tack room and over to a horseshoe-shaped bridle bracket.

"Look!" Whitney held up a new bridle with a full-cheek snaffle bit. "I wanted Apple's name on it—right here." She pointed to the cheekpiece. "But Todd said you just can't do that." She pouted a second, then cocked her head. "Do you like it?"

"It's beautiful." Jina fingered the soft leather. The bridle had a raised cavesson and brow band, and braided reins. All first-class. The Chamberses obviously bought only the best for their daughter.

"Okay, Whitney," her mother said. "We have to get home. I'm expecting a call—"

"No!" Whitney screamed so loudly, Jina's mouth dropped open.

Mrs. Chambers's face flushed. "Whitney," she said, "that wasn't necessary."

Whitney threw the bridle on the floor. "I'm staying here with Jina," she said.

Jina shut her mouth with a surprised snap. She couldn't believe what an incredible brat Whitney was being. She glanced at Mrs. Chambers, not sure what to say.

"Dear, you can't stay here with Jina," Mrs. Chambers said patiently.

"That's right," Jina chimed in. "I'm leaving, too. I'm going back to Foxhall."

"Please take me with you!" Whitney buried her head in Jina's jacket.

Jina wasn't sure what to do. Nervously, Mrs. Chambers smoothed her already perfect hair.

"Whitney," Jina said softly, "you can't come with me to school. I mean, you wouldn't even want to. At night, all we do is homework."

"Homework?" Whitney said suspiciously. "Like spelling words?"

Jina nodded. "We can't even watch TV."

"And I bet Angel made spaghetti for dinner," Mrs. Chambers added.

Whitney glanced from Jina to her mom. "Okay. See you next time, Jina."

"Bye." Jina waved as Whitney went out the

door. Mrs. Chambers threw Jina a relieved smile.

"Thanks," she mouthed as she followed her daughter out the door.

When the two of them had left, Jina blew out her breath. Then she picked up the bridle and hung it up.

What was that all about? she wondered. She didn't know Whitney that well yet, but she had never seen the little girl act so badly.

Whitney seemed to have everything. Except manners.

Jina sighed as she headed out of the tack room.

A bratty horse and a bratty kid.

What had she gotten herself into?

"Boy, am I glad you guys are here!" Andie exclaimed. She sat bolt upright in bed, her hair sticking out everywhere. "What took you so long?"

Jina staggered wearily into the suite. She threw her jacket on the bed, then flopped on her back.

"We were having so much fun at Middlefield!" Lauren said as she bounced through the doorway after Mary Beth. "I never wanted to come back."

Mary Beth giggled. "Yeah, she spent the whole time making googly eyes at Todd." She pulled her sweatshirt over her head. "Sorry you couldn't go with us, Andie."

"No, you're not," Andie said.

Mary Beth dropped her sweatshirt on the

floor. "Gee, you're right," she said.

Andie threw an empty cookie box at her. The top popped open and crumbs scattered everywhere.

Jina groaned. "Andie! I just swept the floor this morning."

"Boy, are you grouchy, Williams," Lauren teased. Bending over, she grabbed one of Jina's black boots and began to pull it off. Mary Beth grabbed the other one.

"Hey!" Jina protested. Her roommates tugged so hard, she slid right off the bed, landing on the floor with a thud.

Mary Beth, Lauren, and Andie burst out laughing. Even Jina had to smile. Sometimes she was sure her roommates were crazy.

"I really did miss you guys," Andie said. "It was so quiet and boring here that I actually studied." She held up several stapled sheets of paper. "I bet you didn't get *this* yet."

"What is it?" Lauren asked.

"A list of all the things we'll need to know for the interschool show."

"What?" Mary Beth snatched the pages and skimmed them quickly. Lauren looked over her shoulder. "It's just a bunch of questions."

Andie nodded. "Right. And we have to

know the answers for the show. Mrs. Caufield says the judges will be testing knowledge as well as riding ability."

Mary Beth groaned. "I've flunked already."

Still on the floor, Jina leaned back against the bed frame. Maybe she should be glad Applejacks wouldn't be ready for the show. It sounded like a lot of hard work. *Stop that!* she scolded herself. Hadn't she agreed to work with the pony in the first place because she wanted to show again?

"You'd better get up, Jina," Mary Beth said. "We've only got five minutes to dress for dinner." She'd already put on her blue Foxhall blazer.

"I'm too tired to go to dinner," Jina said.

"Why?" Lauren asked. "This afternoon was so much fun."

"Fun?" Jina snorted. "Applejacks was a pain, and then Whitney threw a tantrum."

"Whitney threw a tantrum?" Mary Beth asked, sounding shocked.

"No way." Lauren shook her head. "She's an angel." Sitting on the bed, she pulled on navy-blue socks. "I wish she was my sister instead of Stephanie. At least she likes horses."

"Really, Jina," Mary Beth scolded, "first you

complain about Applejacks, then you have to pick on Whitney."

Andie sat up straight. "Wow, sounds like I missed some major excitement at Middlefield. Next time I'm going, too."

Jina rolled her eyes. That would be all she needed.

"So are you coming to dinner or not?" Mary Beth asked Jina again, starting toward the door. "They're having lasagna."

"No. Just bring me a roll," Jina said.

"Oh, good!" Andie's face brightened. "You can stay here with me."

Jina quickly scrambled to her feet. "Actually, lasagna does sound good."

Fifteen minutes later, the three roommates filed into the cafeteria. At dinner Foxhall students had assigned seats that changed every week. That way, Headmaster Frawley had explained, they could get to know all the other girls.

Jina walked around the tables, looking for her name. Finally, she found it. She glanced at the name on the plate next to hers. Ashley Stewart.

"Just my luck," Jina muttered. She couldn't

wait for this lousy day to be over.

Sitting down, she smoothed the white linen napkin on her lap and took a drink of water. A few minutes later, she saw Ashley drift into the cafeteria. Penny was right beside her, as usual. The two of them stopped at Lauren's table.

Jina froze. What were they saying to her roommate now?

Just then, Ashley turned and looked in Jina's direction. Jina snapped her head around. She didn't want Ashley to think she'd been watching her.

"Hi, Jina." Tiffany Dubray sat down on Jina's other side.

"Hi, Tiffany!" Jina said. She sounded so enthusiastic that Tiffany gave her a strange look.

Tiffany was a sixth-grader, too. Jina knew her from two of her classes, English and history. The girl had hair that was so blond it looked white.

"So what are you and your roommates doing for our English project?" Tiffany asked. She had aqua-blue eyes that reminded Jina of pool water.

Jina glanced over her shoulder as Ashley began to cross to the other side of the room.

"Um, I'm not sure. We really haven't talked about it yet."

When Ashley reached her chair without saying anything to her, Jina breathed a sigh of relief. She turned back to Tiffany. "What are you doing for your project?" she asked.

Tiffany shrugged. "Well, I'm not in a group yet, so I was wondering..." Her voice trailed off, and she looked shyly at Jina.

"You want to work with us?" Jina asked as she took the basket of rolls. "Mrs. James said we could have five girls in a group."

Tiffany's eyes brightened. "That'd be great!"

"I'm warning you, though, Andie has been coming up with some pretty strange ideas." Jina began buttering a roll. "After class last week she suggested we do the fight scene from *Romeo and Juliet* using real swords."

"Ooo!" Tiffany said with a silly-sounding giggle. Jina hoped her roommates wouldn't be mad at her for asking Tiffany to join their group.

"Jina, could you please pass the rolls?" Ashley spoke so softly that Jina was startled.

"Uh, sure." Jina took the basket off the table and handed it over to her.

The older girl smiled back. "I hear you had

an interesting time this afternoon at Middlefield," Ashley said as she peeked inside the basket.

Jina almost choked on her roll. *Thanks, Lauren,* she thought. She racked her brain for some clever comeback. There was no way she was going to tell Ashley about her disastrous ride on Applejacks.

"Yes. I had a *very* interesting time," Jina said finally, smiling with false confidence. "Applejacks is one talented pony."

Ashley gazed at her in surprise.

"In fact," Jina continued, "I think he's going to clean up at the winter shows. Let's see—" she tapped her forehead, pretending to think hard "—the first indoor show is in a few weeks, right? Like you said before, I'll see you there."

Jina coolly dug into her salad, waiting for a snotty retort. But Ashley didn't say a word.

Maybe Todd was right, Jina thought. Maybe dealing with Applejacks would be good for her after all.

She was beginning to feel a whole lot tougher.

"Act out a *fairy* tale?" Andie wrinkled her nose at Jina. "That's a lame idea, Williams."

It was the next day in English class, and everyone was meeting in their project groups. The roommates and Tiffany had pulled their chairs into a circle in the far corner of the room.

"Jina's idea is *not* dumb," Lauren protested. "We did that unit on fairy tales two weeks ago. It was fun."

Jina smiled gratefully at Lauren. Andie was still mad at her for asking Tiffany to join their group. It wasn't so much that Andie had any reason not to like Tiffany, but ever since her last fiasco with Magic, Andie was angry at the world.

Andie crossed her arms in front of her chest. Her wrapped knee was sticking out in the middle of the circle, and her crutches were propped against the chair seat. "I don't like those dumb fairy tales. The princesses are always such wimps."

"I agree," Mary Beth piped up. "Some handsome prince always has to save them with a kiss or something."

Lauren nudged Andie with her elbow. "Mary Beth must be thinking about *Tommy*."

"Or maybe *Brad*," Andie teased.

Mary Beth's face turned so red that her freckles disappeared. Jina hid a smile behind her notebook. It was hard to believe Mary Beth had two boyfriends.

"Do you—kind of, anyway—mean Tommy Isaacson from Manchester School?" Tiffany asked.

Andie raised one eyebrow. "Didn't you dance with him at the farewell dinner? Remember? Mary Beth was so jealous."

"Andie!" Mary Beth protested. "You're making that up."

"So, girls, you seem to be having a spirited discussion," Mrs. James said, appearing suddenly behind Jina. Their English teacher was a tall, handsome woman with chocolate-colored skin and broad shoulders.

Oops. Ducking her chin, Jina busily wrote "English Project Ideas" in her notebook.

"Oh, we are," Andie spoke up. "No one agrees on what we should do for our project."

"Well, since you all like horses so much, why not go with something like that?" Mrs. James suggested.

At first, no one said anything. Everyone looked confused.

"You mean like ride a horse onstage?" Lauren asked finally.

Mrs. James laughed. "No, I mean look at some literature that has a horse theme. Maybe you could turn a chapter of a book into a play and act it out." She smiled and moved on to another group.

"That's not a bad idea," Mary Beth said.

Andie snorted. "Yeah. We'll do *The Black Stallion.* Tiffany can play the horse's rear end."

The whole group cracked up. Jina had to clap her hand over her mouth so she wouldn't laugh too loud. Tiffany was giggling too, even though Jina thought it sounded kind of forced.

Mrs. James shot them a withering look. "Discuss quietly, girls!"

Jina choked back her laughter. She didn't want to get in trouble with Mrs. James. English was her favorite subject.

A few weeks earlier, back when she'd been showing Superstar, she'd been under so much pressure she hadn't had time to enjoy her English class. Now when she was assigned books to read, she could relax and really get into them.

"What about a scene from *Black Beauty*?" Lauren suggested. "That's a classic."

"Okay." Andie flipped her hair behind her shoulders. "We can do the part where Beauty almost dies. I'll be the one who saves her."

"Him," Lauren corrected. "Beauty was a him."

Mary Beth shook her head. "No way. I'm not acting out a scene where a horse gets sick."

"Well, most of the scenes in *Black Beauty* are sad," Lauren said. "Didn't you ever read the book, Mary Beth?"

Mary Beth looked down at her desk. "No. I wasn't into horses like you guys."

"Why don't we all read the book?" Jina said. "Then we can vote on a chapter."

"Okay, let's vote on a chapter," Tiffany agreed, nodding.

Andie frowned at her. "You sound like a parrot, Tiffany." She squawked and flapped her arms.

Tiffany blushed. Jina wished Andie would quit picking on her. Maybe Tiffany did try too hard to fit in sometimes, but she was a nice person.

Jina stood up. "I'll ask Mrs. James if she has any copies of *Black Beauty*. We can get others from the school library."

"Why don't we skim through the book, then meet tomorrow night after study hours and discuss it?" Mary Beth suggested.

"You guys read it," Andie said. She stretched her arms high and yawned. "I've got too much makeup work to finish." She grinned up at Jina. "Besides, since I can't ride yet, I've decided to go to Middlefield tomorrow and watch Rich Girl here get bucked off Rotten Apple."

"What do you mean?" Jina blurted.

"I don't have anything better to do," Andie explained, "and compared to boring Foxhall, Middlefield sounds so much more exciting."

I don't want you to go with me! Jina wanted to shout. Instead, she just glowered at Andie. If Andie came to watch and she *did* get bucked off Applejacks, her roommate would never let her forget it.

"*This* is the horrible monster that's been trying to buck you off?" Andie asked Jina in disbelief.

It was Wednesday afternoon, and the two girls were standing outside Applejacks's stall.

Jina nodded, grasping the halter and lead more tightly. She just knew Andie was going to make fun of her all afternoon.

Andie shifted her weight on her crutches. Then she stuck her fingers through the wire mesh and wiggled them. "Come here, you fiendish creature."

Ears pricked up, Applejacks came over and lipped her fingers gently. Andie chuckled. "He sure is vicious."

"Look, Andie," Jina said firmly, "I've got to brush him and tack him up. So if you don't mind, there are plenty of other things for you to see at Middlefield."

"Yeah, but I'd rather watch you ride old Killer here," Andie joked.

Jina took a deep breath, trying to stay calm. Sometimes she felt like punching Andie.

When she'd arrived at Middlefield, Todd

had told her that Applejacks had gone perfectly yesterday.

That means it's your fault if things don't go well today, Jina told herself. But she still didn't have a clue what she was doing wrong. And she didn't need Andie rubbing it in.

She'd looked through all her horse books and magazines last night. There had been tons of advice on lameness, illnesses, showing, and jumping.

None had said anything about cranky ponies who just didn't like you.

"Hey, Jina," Andie said, "who is that *gorgeous* creature?"

Jina turned around.

Jazz Man was standing in crossties, his chestnut coat gleaming.

"That's the horse that won the Volvo World Cup Finals," Jina said.

"No, dummy. Not the *horse*. I mean the guy who's grooming him."

Jina looked closer. A blond boy about fifteen was bent over, brushing Jazz Man's front leg. It was Spencer. "That's Todd's younger brother," she said.

Andie's brows shot up. "*Todd* has a younger brother?"

"Yep. His name's Spencer. He's a working student at Middlefield. He goes to high school near here, so he comes in the afternoons."

"You didn't tell me," Andie said accusingly.

Jina frowned. "Tell you what?"

"All about him!" Andie shook her head. "I can't believe you, Williams. Todd has a gorgeous younger brother and you never even mention it. Some friend you are." She smoothed her hair. "How do I look?"

"Fine," Jina said, shrugging.

"Good. I'm going to introduce myself to Spencer. He's got a weird name, but he looks okay. *More* than okay."

Without a backward glance, Andie swung down the aisle on her crutches.

Jina smiled to herself. Finally Andie was gone. Now she could get Applejacks ready. And she had to hurry before Todd chewed her out for taking so long.

Reaching in her pocket, Jina pulled out a carrot, an apple, and a handful of horse treats. All bribes. She hoped Applejacks liked one of them.

He loved all three.

While the pony munched half the apple, Jina unbuckled his blanket, slid it off, and hung it over the top of the stall door. For a moment, she considered leading him into the aisle and hooking him to the crossties.

She peeked out the stall door. Andie was propped on her crutches, busily talking to Spencer. He was picking out Jazz Man's hooves, nodding as he listened to her.

Jina popped her head back in. *We'd better stay in the stall,* she decided. *That way, if Applejacks does something dumb, no one else will see.*

"It's just you and me, buddy," she said, turning back to the pony. She tossed the other half of the apple into his feed tub. "We're making friends, right?"

He ducked his head into the tub and crunched noisily. While he ate, she brushed him, then picked out his hooves.

With one hand on the lead rope, Jina reached around the doorway for her saddle and pad. Carefully, she set them on his back, then smoothed the pad under the saddle.

She walked around Applejacks's head to his other side and made sure the girth was straight. When she walked back, she scratched his forehead. He wiggled his upper lip happily.

So far, so good.

But when she reached for the girth, Applejacks turned and stared at her. His ears were flat against his head.

"I know, you don't like this part," Jina said, trying not to sound even a teeny bit nervous "I'll tighten the girth little by little. You won't even notice. Okay?"

Apple's ears flicked back and forth. He shook his head, his mane flying, as if to say no.

Butterflies churned in Jina's stomach. Grabbing the end of the girth, she slid the straps through the buckles. Suddenly, without warning, Applejacks snaked his head around.

His mouth wide open, the pony sunk his teeth deep into Jina's wrist!

Jina heard a crunch. Then she screamed, as pain shot up her left arm.

Blindly, she whacked at Applejacks with her other hand. He threw up his head and backed into a corner. Jina grabbed her wrist.

Gritting her teeth against the pain, she rolled up her jacket sleeve, just as Andie flung open the stall door. Spencer was right behind her.

"What's wrong?" Andie asked breathlessly. She was balancing awkwardly on her crutches. "We heard you scream."

"Nothing's wrong." Jina shoved her hand into her jacket pocket. "Apple stepped on my foot, that's all," she fibbed. "It just surprised me."

Andie frowned at her, then at Applejacks.

The pony stood quietly in the corner, his ears flat as if he knew he'd done something wrong.

"Is anything broken?" Spencer asked. He was slender and blue-eyed like Todd.

Jina wiggled her toes in her boot and pretended to think. Her wrist was killing her. And what had made that awful crunch?

"No, nothing's broken." She tried to smile convincingly.

"Good," Spencer said. "I guess you were lucky."

"Well, if you're sure you're all right, Williams, I'm going to help Spencer clean tack." Andie hesitated, then hobbled out of the stall after Spencer.

As soon as they'd left, Jina pulled her hand from her pocket. Gingerly, she pushed up the sleeve of her turtleneck, expecting to see crushed bones.

Instead, she saw a huge black and blue bruise and a mangled plastic watch face. Jina sighed with relief. She'd forgotten she'd been wearing her wristwatch. That's what had crunched.

"Jina?"

Jina spun around. Todd was staring strangely at her. His gaze dropped to her wrist.

"What in the world happened to you?" Todd strode into the stall. Frowning, he looked at Jina's wrist, then at Jina. She couldn't meet his eyes.

"Nothing," Jina whispered, trying not to cry. Everything was such a mess. Why had she ever decided to ride this mean, stupid pony?

"Nothing?" Todd repeated in disbelief. "Big bite marks are *nothing*?"

Jina put her hand behind her back. "It doesn't hurt and it was my fault. I should have put Apple in crossties. Then he couldn't have bitten me."

For a moment, Todd didn't say anything. But Jina knew what he was thinking—that he'd made a big mistake asking her to work with a green pony. She was a failure.

"You're right," Todd said, after what seemed like forever. "You should have put him in crossties. Go run cold water on your wrist. I'll tack Applejacks up."

Jina unclasped the broken watch and stuck it in her jacket pocket. "No, I've got to finish saddling him myself. Just hold his head for me, please."

Todd nodded. He grabbed hold of the dangling lead and brought the pony forward. Jina took a deep breath, grabbed the girth, and tightened it.

Applejacks pinned back his ears but didn't move.

Without looking at Todd, Jina slid the reins over Apple's head. Then she unbuckled the halter and quickly bridled the pony, ignoring his big teeth as she slid the bit into his mouth.

"Jina, you don't need to do this," Todd said quietly.

Jina shoved her helmet on her head. "Yes, I do." Tears filled her eyes. Quickly, she wiped them away so Todd wouldn't see.

The trainer led Applejacks from the stall. Jina followed him down the aisle.

"Jina! Todd! Apple!" Whitney burst from the tack room. Mrs. Chambers was right behind her daughter. She was wearing a gray wool suit with a pale pink blouse.

"Whitney wanted to come early to watch you ride, Jina," Mrs. Chambers explained with an apologetic smile. "Her father will pick her up in an hour."

Whitney spun around to face her mother. "I don't want Dad to pick me up!" she said.

Mrs. Chambers pursed her lips. "Honey, you know I have a meeting tonight, and—"

"So don't go!" Whitney demanded. Jina couldn't believe what she was hearing. Whitney was worse than a brat! Her own mother would never let her get away with talking like this.

"Hey, Whitney," Todd said, "didn't you want a lesson on Polo today—cantering?"

Whitney's face suddenly brightened. "Canter Polo? Cool!"

"What a fantastic idea." Mrs. Chambers sounded extremely relieved. "'Bye, sweetie," she said to Whitney. "Have a good lesson."

Whitney just nodded and turned to Jina. "Hey, maybe you can canter Apple today." Digging in her pocket, she pulled out a carrot.

"Whitney, don't feed Apple when he has the bridle on," Jina warned.

Whitney held the carrot out anyway. Before Applejacks could take it, Jina snatched it from Whitney's palm. She knew horses could choke if they ate with a bit in their mouth.

"Hey!" Whitney grabbed the carrot right back and defiantly held it out to Applejacks.

Todd put his hand on Jina's arm. "Let her give it to him, Jina," he said in a low voice. "It'll be okay."

Whitney grinned happily as Applejacks

crunched the carrot. "See? He likes it."

Jina turned away. No wonder Whitney was so spoiled. It seemed as if everybody gave in to her demands.

"We'd better get moving if you're both going to ride," Todd said, clucking to Applejacks.

Whitney took Jina's hand in hers. "I'm so glad I came to watch."

When they reached the indoor arena, Whitney ran up the concrete steps that led to a small section of bleachers. Several other people were already there, watching riders school their horses.

Jina clenched her jaw. *An audience*. Just what she needed.

Stop it, she told herself. *You're used to having people watch you ride*.

Todd gave her a leg up. Jina squared her body in the saddle and picked up the reins. Applejacks swished his tail.

"I'm going to shorten your stirrups," Todd said as he lifted the saddle flap. "Whitney is smaller than you. I think maybe your longer legs against Apple's sides are causing him to be so jumpy."

Jina nodded, glad that Todd had at least

come up with a possible reason. "Let's hope so."

When Todd finished raising both stirrups, Jina squeezed Apple gently with her calves. Applejacks strode off in a stiff-legged walk. The short stirrups made Jina feel even more awkward.

"Make a big circle around me," Todd said. "And give him more leg. I want to see longer, freer strides."

Jina nodded. But when she pressed her heels against the pony's sides, he flattened his ears and crow-hopped.

Jina groaned. It was happening again!

She steered Apple around one end of the arena, as far from the other riders as possible. When the pony finally settled into a smoother walk, Todd told them to trot.

Jina signaled Applejacks. Ears pinned back, he ducked his head and tried to buck. Jina pulled hard on the right rein, forcing his head up.

"Make him go forward!" Todd yelled, his tone angry. "Don't let him boss you, Jina!"

She dug her heels into his sides. Apple danced sideways, resisting. His back was hollow, his neck bent in a stiff arc.

Jina pulled the rebellious pony to a sharp halt right in front of the stands.

"What's the matter, Jina?" Whitney called. Jina glanced up. She'd forgotten about Whitney. The little girl was hanging over the arena wall.

"Can't you get him to trot?" Whitney asked.

Does it look like I can? Jina answered silently. What would she do if this were Superstar? But Superstar had never acted like this stubborn, balky pony.

"Todd, I want to ride Applejacks now," Whitney whined, her voice loud enough for everyone to hear. "Jina can't even get him to trot."

"Shut up, Whitney," Jina muttered. The whole world didn't need to know what a hard time she was having with a little pony, even if he was green.

"Just a minute, Whitney," Todd said. He strode up to Jina. "What do you want to do?" he asked her.

"I'm not sure," Jina admitted. "I don't want to just give up, but—"

"I want to ride him *now*!" Jumping off the steps, Whitney raced across the arena. "Jina's not such a great rider. I can ride him better than her!"

Jina stiffened. Whitney was being really rude, but she was right.

Quickly, Jina dismounted and unbuckled the girth. "Let her ride him," she told Todd. "Obviously I can't."

Before Todd could reply, Jina yanked off her saddle and pad, then walked out of the arena. She knew all eyes were on her so she held her head high.

But when Jina reached Applejacks's stall, she dropped into a dark corner and hid her face in her hands.

Why can't I ride Applejacks? Why does he hate me so much?

Jina stayed in the stall for a long time. Finally she emerged, determined to keep things together. She was tired of feeling sorry for herself.

Glancing at the stable clock, she headed for the tack room to find Andie. Foxhall's minibus was scheduled to pick them up any minute.

"Hey, Jina!" Whitney was coming down the aisle, leading Applejacks by the reins. She grinned widely. "Apple and I had a great ride."

"That's nice," Jina said flatly.

Whitney halted the pony. "Only now Todd says I have to cool him off."

Jina felt the pony's neck. It was sweaty and warm. "That's right. If he's hot when you put him in his stall, he might get sick."

"Well, I hate to cool off horses." Whitney pouted. "It's too much work." Peeking up at Jina, she smiled sweetly. "Will you do it for me? You rode him, too."

Jina sighed and reached for the reins. "I'll help. But remember, a big part of riding is caring for your horse."

"Not me. I'm going to have grooms to do it," Whitney said. "You're my groom right now!"

Jina looked sharply at Whitney, her jaw tightening. She was trying hard to be nice, but any second...

"I'm going to get a soda," Whitney said. "I'll see you later."

"Oh, no, you don't." Jina grabbed the little girl's shirt. "Not until Apple is cooled off."

Whitney tried to pull away. "Ow! You're hurting me!"

Bending over, Jina looked directly into Whitney's big blue eyes. "I'm not hurting you," she said calmly. "I'm going to let you go, and then we'll untack Applejacks together."

Whitney glared at her, her face red with anger. Slowly, Jina released her grasp.

Whitney instantly scrambled backward. "I will not untack him!" she screamed. "I hate you, Jina Williams! You're a terrible rider, and when my father comes I'm telling him that you're not my friend anymore and I never want to see you again!"

Jina threw up her hands as the little girl ran off down the aisle, pigtails flying. She couldn't decide who was more obnoxious: Applejacks or Whitney.

"Spencer is even *cuter* than Todd," Andie declared that night. She was lying on her bed, an open book propped on her stomach.

Jina plugged her ears with her fingers. She was trying to finish her history homework. Besides, she was sick of hearing about Spencer and Middlefield. She wanted to forget everything about the whole miserable afternoon.

Lauren obviously wasn't sick of those subjects. For the past fifteen minutes, she'd been listening intently to Andie, her math homework untouched on the desk in front of her.

"You said he looked just like Todd," Lauren said, "so how can he be cuter?"

Andie grinned at her. "Well, they both do have gorgeous blond hair, awesome blue eyes, and amazing bods, but Spencer's *younger*. He's absolutely perfect for me."

"Hey, guys," Mary Beth interrupted. She was hunched on her bed, reading a book. "After study hours are over, Tiffany's coming here to talk about *Black Beauty*. Am I the only one who has homework to finish?"

Thank you, Mary Beth, Jina said silently. At least one other person in the suite had her mind on other things—like school.

Then Mary Beth added, "Tommy's calling at nine-thirty, so I want to done before then." Jina rolled her eyes to the ceiling. Was she the only one in the suite who wasn't boy crazy?

"Ask Mr. Wimpy if he's going to be at the interschool show," Andie said.

Lauren glanced down at Jina, who was sitting on the floor. "Hey, do you think Spencer will be there? I'd love to see what he looks like."

Jina slammed her history book shut. "No, I don't think Spencer will be there. Use your head, Lauren. Middlefield is a *stable*, not a *school*. Besides, a lot of riders will all be at the last A-rated show, trying to win points. It's the same weekend, in case you didn't know." *And that show is where I'd be if Superstar weren't lame,* she added to herself. Abruptly, she jumped up.

Lauren's face crumpled. "Sorry. I forgot."

Jina didn't reply. She knew Lauren didn't deserve such a nasty retort. She was just mad at *everybody.*

Grabbing her shower bucket, Jina stomped into the bathroom. As she slammed the door shut, she heard Lauren say in a low voice, "What's wrong with *her?*"

Everything! Jina wanted to yell out the door. The whole week stunk. It just wasn't fair, she decided as she dumped her bucket on the counter. If Superstar hadn't gone lame, she never would have met bratty Whitney and her stupid pony.

What she needed was to buy another horse, one she could show until Superstar was healed. When Superstar went lame, her mother had offered, but Jina hadn't been interested. Maybe she should have given the idea more thought.

"Jina?" Someone rapped on the door.

"Tiffany's here."

Jina sighed. "I'll be right out."

She combed her hair, still thinking. Todd and Mrs. Caufield could help her look for a horse this winter. They'd get another Superstar—a young but well-trained horse with manners, conformation, and tons of talent. *I might even win the Junior Horse of the Year Award again*, Jina thought.

She opened the bathroom door, feeling better. Tiffany was sitting on the end of Jina's bed. She was staring at Mary Beth, who was sobbing loudly on the floor.

"What's wrong?" Jina asked in alarm, rushing over to Mary Beth. Lauren sat next to her on the bed, her arm around Mary Beth's shoulder. *Black Beauty* lay facedown in Mary Beth's lap.

Lauren looked up. "We don't know."

"Are you all right?" Jina asked Mary Beth, sitting down on her other side. "Did you get a letter from your parents? Has something terrible happened? Is it Tommy?"

"No-o-o!" Mary Beth wailed. "It's—it's—Ginger."

"Ginger?" Jina repeated, puzzled. She looked at the others. They all shrugged in confusion.

"Who's Ginger?" Lauren asked gently.

"The horse," Mary Beth choked out as fresh tears streamed down her cheeks. "Black Beauty's friend." She wiped her nose on her sleeve. "She died and Beauty saw her in the back of the cart. Her eyes were all sunken and—and—it was *awful!*"

Andie snorted. "You're crying over a character in a book?" She shook her head in disbelief. "Finney, you are such a wimp."

Lauren scowled at Andie. "She's not a wimp. It *was* sad."

Tiffany handed Mary Beth the box of tissues off Jina's desk. "Hey, I even cried, too," she said. "And I don't even like horses."

"See, I told you guys Tiffany was weird," Andie muttered to Lauren.

Mary Beth dried her tears, then blew her nose loudly. "Better?" Jina patted Mary Beth's arm. She nodded and blew her nose again.

Lauren picked up the book. "Okay, so are we ready to discuss how to turn *Black Beauty* into our English project?"

"There don't seem to be any scenes for five people," Tiffany piped up. "I mean, it's mostly horses talking."

"That's why we should turn it into a play," Andie said. "The dialogue will be easy. 'Neigh, neigh, whinny.' I can handle that."

"Well, I don't want to play a *horse*," Tiffany said. "Isn't there some human part?"

"Come on, Tiffany," Andie said. "You'd make a perfect Merrylegs."

Tiffany frowned and bit a fingernail. "Merry-legs? Wasn't that the fat pony?"

Andie just grinned.

"I have a suggestion," Jina said suddenly. "Not all of the other girls in our English class are riders, so a lot of them don't know much about horses. We could combine some of the scenes in the book that show what to do and what not to do when you care for horses."

No one said anything.

"Huh?" Lauren said.

"You know," Jina continued, her enthusiasm growing. "Like when Beauty has to race to the doctor's house to save his mistress. He's all hot when he comes back to the stable and the groom doesn't cool him down right and gives him a full pail of water so he gets real sick. If we did it like a play, Beauty could be telling another horse what the groom did wrong." Jina glanced eagerly at her roommates. "So what do you think?"

Tiffany was leaning forward on the bed, bit-ing her nails. Andie had pulled a hunk of wild, curly hair in front of her face and was checking for split ends. Mary Beth and Lauren began to flip through the pages of the book.

"Uh—" Tiffany began. She glanced nervously at the others as if she didn't want to say anything until they did.

Jina could tell her roommates hated her idea.

"All right, so we won't do that." Now she felt stupid.

"No, I like the idea," Lauren said. "It would be fun being a horse." She shook her head and pawed the bed with her fist as if it were a hoof.

Andie flopped back on her pillow. "I don't really care what we do so long as I get an A. Do you think your brilliant idea will get us an A, Williams?"

Jina pressed her lips together. She could feel a headache beginning behind her eyes. "How should I know?"

"I bet it would," Tiffany chimed in. "Mrs. James likes everything Jina does."

"Teacher's pet," Andie sang out.

Ignoring her, Jina got up and pulled her nightgown from the drawer. She wished her roommates would disappear so she could go to bed.

"Well, I refuse to be Ginger," Mary Beth declared.

"But you'd make a perfect Ginger with your red hair," Tiffany pointed out.

Andie chuckled. "And with your looks, you'll be the best at playing dead." She hung her tongue from her mouth and rolled her eyes up under her lids.

Mary Beth threw a pillow at one another. "That's gross, Andie."

Suddenly, everyone was throwing pillows at each other. Even Jina joined in. Just then the door of the suite opened and Ellie, one of the girls from 4C, stuck her head in. She ducked as a pillow narrowly missed her.

"Hey, Jina," Ellie said, "telephone."

Jina snapped to attention. Her mom!

She dropped the pillow she was holding onto the bed and raced to the phone in the hall. "Hi, Mom!" she said, grabbing the receiver. "Guess what? I've decided we should buy a new horse!" she blurted excitedly.

"Oh, honey, I'm so glad!" her mother exclaimed. "What made you change your mind?"

"Well, Superstar's getting better, but it will be at least a month or two before I can ride him," Jina replied. "That means he'll never be ready for the spring shows. If I want to work toward a Zone Award next year, I'll need another horse."

"Well, I think it's a wonderful idea," her mother said. "Especially since I thought of it in the first place."

Jina grinned into the receiver.

"We'll get you the best horse in the world," her mom continued. "Then you can show this spring and be a winner again!"

Be a winner again.

Jina's fingers tensed on the receiver, and her mouth suddenly went dry.

What had Ashley Stewart said only a month ago? "*Anyone could win riding a fifty-thousand-dollar horse. Even a lousy rider like you!*"

Is that what everyone would think? Even her own mother believed that Jina could only be a winner if she had a million-dollar horse. She had to buy her daughter's champion ribbons and trophies.

A cold knot formed in Jina's stomach. Then she dropped the phone and doubled over, feeling sick.

"Jina are you still there?" Myra Golden's voice called from the end of the dangling receiver.

Slowly, Jina reached down to pick it up. "I'm here," she whispered.

"I'll call Mrs. Caufield first, then Todd," her mother babbled happily. "I'm sure they'll know just where to find the best horse for my girl."

"No, Mom. I've changed my mind." Jina took a deep breath as she straightened up. Her cheeks felt burning hot. "I've already got the greatest horse in the world."

"I know that, honey," her mother's voice said soothingly, "but there's no reason you can't have *two* wonderful horses."

Jina shook her head emphatically, even though she knew her mother couldn't see her. "No. Forget what I said. It was a lousy idea.

Look, I've got to go. I'll talk to you soon, okay? 'Bye."

"Jina?" She could hear the question in her mother's voice as she hung up.

Jina leaned back against the wall and shut her eyes. Her stomach was still churning. She really did feel sick. She had finally realized what everyone else had known all along: that Jina Williams wasn't really a winner. It was only the horses she rode that had made her a champion.

"Jina?" Someone was shaking her shoulder. Jina's eyes flew open. She was in bed, in her nightgown.

Lauren bent over her, frowning. "You slept through your alarm. I didn't want you to be late for class."

"What time is it?" Jina rubbed her temples. Her head was pounding.

"Five minutes to eight." Lauren sat on the edge of the bed. "I had to come back to the suite to get my math notebook. Your alarm was buzzing like crazy."

Jina propped herself up on her elbows. The light from the window hurt her eyes. She couldn't believe it was morning already. And she couldn't remember having gone to bed.

"Jina, are you all right?" Lauren asked. She placed her palm on Jina's forehead and clucked like a mother hen. "I think you've got a fever."

"No, I'm all right." Jina sat up and swung her legs to the floor. Instantly her stomach heaved.

With a groan, she fell back on her pillow. "Maybe I'm not."

Lauren stood up. "I'll get Ms. Shiroo." She tucked the quilt under Jina's chin, then dashed from the suite.

Jina shut her eyes. She really did feel miserable. Maybe that's why she'd been doing everything wrong all week: because she was getting sick.

Twenty minutes later, Ms. Shiroo, the dorm mother, had summoned Mrs. Zelinski, the school nurse. Jina soon had a cool washcloth on her forehead, a throw-up pan by the bed, and a thermometer stuck in her mouth.

Mrs. Zelinski was tall and heavy with very noticeable black mustache hairs. Wistfully, Jina thought of Grandma Williams, who had always come to stay with her when Jina was sick. She was small and trim with her gray hair tucked in a bun. For hours she'd sit by Jina's bed, her cool hands smoothing back her hair. She'd sing hymns and read Jina's favorite books to her all night long.

"Well, Miss Williams," Nurse Zelinski's voice boomed heartily as she pulled the thermometer out from under Jina's tongue. "Your temperature is 101. I'm afraid you've caught that awful twenty-four-hour flu that's spreading through the campus."

Jina groaned. *The flu.* At least she could have caught something a little more interesting.

"I want you to rest now, I've got a dozen other girls who are sick, too, so I can't move you into the infirmary yet. But I'll come to check on you later."

Jina nodded, and her eyelids fluttered shut.

When she awoke the second time, the suite was quiet. Her hair was damp with sweat and her nightgown, pillows, and sheets felt soggy. She kicked off the quilt, trying to get cool.

"Hey, quit that," someone said.

Jina lifted her head. Mary Beth was getting up from her desk chair. Her brows were knit together in a look of concern.

"I'm all sweaty," Jina croaked.

"It sounds like your fever broke." Mary Beth picked up a glass of chipped ice. "Try a little of this. Then I'll change your sheets."

As Jina sucked on the ice, she looked gratefully at Mary Beth. "Thanks a lot," she said. "But why are you here playing nurse? Aren't you missing class?"

"Nope. It's almost five o'clock," Mary Beth said, sitting down at her desk again. "I took a break from riding today to study those questions for the horse show. Sometimes I just get so *discouraged*. There's so much to learn."

"But you've been doing so much better lately," Jina said.

Mary Beth smiled grimly. "Not *that* much better. I won't even be cantering by the time we go to the interschool show. I'm going to have to enter the walk-trot class!"

"So?" Jina slumped back on her pillow.

"So, Tommy will think I'm a dork."

"No, he won't." Jina shut her eyes. "He'll know you're trying your best."

Which is what I need to do, Jina added to herself. She had to figure out how to ride Applejacks. She had to prove to everyone she wasn't a lousy rider.

Mary Beth went over and rummaged

through Jina's dresser drawers until she found a clean nightgown. "Is this okay? You need to get out of that sweaty one."

Jina nodded. "How do you know so much about taking care of sick people?"

Mary Beth chuckled. "I have three younger brothers and sisters, remember?"

"Oh." Jina sat up. She felt a little dizzy but the headache was gone. Mary Beth helped her into the bathroom where she changed and splashed cool water on her face.

When she came out, Mary Beth was smoothing the quilt over fresh sheets. "Ready for Mrs. Zelinski and her chicken soup?"

"I guess." Jina slid back under the covers. It was great to feel so much better. "Would you please hand me that stack of horse magazines?" She pointed to a pile by Andie's bed. "I've got to figure out how to handle Applejacks."

Mary Beth gave her a strange look. "What's wrong with him?" she asked, handing her the magazines.

Jina bit her lip. Maybe Mary Beth would understand. She had to talk to *someone*.

"I don't think there's anything wrong with *Applejacks*," Jina admitted reluctantly. "It's *me*.

For some reason, he doesn't like me." She began to flip through the first magazine. "But I'm going to figure out what I'm doing wrong—and fix it!"

Oh, Superstar, you are the greatest, Jina thought wistfully. She was leaning on the top rail of the paddock, watching the handsome gray. He wasn't doing anything exciting—just picking around at the grass—but she didn't care. He was still the best. And Superstar loved her.

It was Friday afternoon. Jina had felt well enough to go to classes, but she'd skipped her lesson at Middlefield. She was still a little weak, but the main reason she hadn't wanted to go was that she still didn't know what to do about Applejacks.

And she didn't think she could stand one more humiliating ride.

Unlatching the gate, Jina whistled. Superstar popped his head up, nickered, and trotted over. She snapped the lead onto his halter and opened the gate wide. She'd give him a good brushing before his dinner.

When they reached the new barn, Jina hooked the Thoroughbred to crossties, then curried him all over. He wiggled his upper lip, loving every stroke. She laughed and patted his neck.

Because they weren't going to shows lately, Superstar hadn't been clipped. This was the first year his winter coat had grown, and he felt as soft and fuzzy as a teddy bear.

"And you're as fat as one, too!" Jina scolded. Stepping back, she checked out the horse's hay belly. He'd been in such good shape all year. But since he hadn't been worked for over a month, his muscles were losing their tone.

Jina glanced down at his right leg. It looked perfectly normal, but the ultrasound Dr. Holden had performed just last week showed that the tendons were still healing.

As Jina brushed out his tail, Superstar began to bob his head excitedly. Dorothy, the stable manager, was walking down the aisle, a bucket swinging by her side.

Superstar bellowed.

"Hungry?" Dorothy chuckled. She was short with wide hips, and she wore a sweatshirt that said A WOMAN'S PLACE IS ON A HORSE. Dorothy had a lot of sweatshirts like that.

"Maybe you need to cut out some of his grain," Jina said, patting Superstar's belly.

"Oh, he's all right. That'll come off once you start riding again." Dorothy poured the sweet feed into Superstar's tub. He shook his head and pawed, eager to eat.

Laughing, Jina unhooked the crossties. The Thoroughbred hurried into the stall, stuck his head into his tub, and sprayed feed everywhere.

"Pig." Jina pulled his blanket off the door and threw it over his back.

Dorothy leaned against the doorjamb. "So are you taking Superstar to the interschool show?"

Jina shook her head. "You know I can't ride him."

"Maybe not, but they're having a fitting and showing class."

"What's that?" Jina asked.

"It's when your horse is judged on how well he's presented—tack, grooming—that kind of stuff. Ask Mrs. Caufield to show you the list of classes." Suddenly, the stable manager snapped her fingers. "That reminds me. Mrs. Caufield needs to see you."

"She does?" Jina said in surprise.

"She should be in the office right now," Dorothy added. "You can probably catch her there before dinner."

"Okay." Jina watched as Dorothy moved on down the aisle to another stall. What did Mrs. Caufield want? she wondered. Was it something about Superstar? Maybe Dr. Holden had something new to report about the Thoroughbred's leg.

Quickly, she finished buckling Superstar's blanket. Then she hurried across the courtyard in front of Foxhall's older barn. The sun was starting to set, and the night air was cool. Tomorrow, there would be frost on the grass.

When Jina reached the barn office, she knocked on the door.

"Come in!"

She opened the door and peeked in. Mrs. Caufield was sitting in her desk chair, drinking a bottle of soda. Her dirt-caked paddock boots were up on the top of her desk, and her gray-streaked hair was pulled back in a hastily clasped barrette.

She waved Jina inside. "I have got something to discuss with you, Jina," the riding director said. She sounded very serious.

Jina's heart flip-flopped. *Superstar!* she thought frantically. Had Dr. Holden discovered something else wrong?

"I just had a call from Todd."

Jina frowned. What did her trainer want? Was he upset that she had skipped her lesson?

"I'm afraid he wanted me to give you some bad news." Mrs. Caufield set her legs back on the ground.

"Bad news?" Jina repeated, her voice shaking. Had there been an accident at Middlefield?

"Todd just finished talking to the Chamberses," Mrs. Caufield said. She leaned forward in her chair. "The family has decided they don't want you to ride Applejacks anymore."

"The Chamberses don't want me to ride Applejacks?" Jina repeated in shocked surprise. "Why not?"

Mrs. Caufield fiddled with a pen on her desk. "It seems Whitney told her father that she didn't want you riding him anymore."

Whitney! Jina should have known. "Well, she's right about one thing," Jina said slowly, her face burning with humiliation. "Applejacks and I don't get along."

"That's what Todd said." Mrs. Caufield leaned back in her chair. "What do *you* think the problem is?"

Jina dropped her gaze to her feet. "I'm just not a good enough rider, I guess."

Mrs. Caufield snorted, and Jina heard the sudden scrape of chair legs on the tile floor.

"That's baloney. You're one of the best riders at Foxhall, and you know it."

Jina shook her head. "No. I'm only the best when I'm on a winning horse." She choked back a sob. "Applejacks is green—and I just can't handle him."

For a moment, Mrs. Caufield didn't say anything. Jina peered up at her through tear-filled eyes. The riding director was twirling her pen and frowning.

"Well, one thing's for sure," Mrs. Caufield said finally. "That pony has sure trampled your self-confidence. I'm going to call Todd and have him bring Applejacks to Foxhall. Saturday afternoon. I want to watch you ride him. I want to see for myself what's going on."

Jina nodded miserably.

The director stood up. "You're a talented rider, Jina Williams. But my telling you that isn't going to mean anything if *you* don't believe it."

Jina nodded again, not sure what to say.

"By the way, we've scheduled a trail ride for tomorrow morning. Everybody—riders and horses—needs to get out of the ring for a change. I've assigned you Lukas."

Lukas?

Jina's mouth dropped open. Lukas was a nervous Anglo-Arabian who shied at his own shadow. All the students had trouble riding him.

Thanks a lot, Mrs. Caufield. Then it dawned on Jina that the riding director had assigned Lukas to her because she knew that Jina could handle him.

A glimmer of hope fluttered inside Jina. She just had to trust that Mrs. Caufield was right.

"This was a great idea," Lauren said the next morning. She and Whisper were walking down an old logging road next to Jina and Lukas. Mary Beth and Andie, her knee well enough now to ride, rode ahead of them with Katherine Parks, the dressage instructor, and several other Foxhall riders.

"I think so, too." Jina patted Lukas on the neck. The gelding was so light-colored he was almost white. So far, he was actually behaving.

A branch snapped suddenly in the woods beside them, and Lukas skittered sideways. Jina sat deep in the saddle and quietly steered him away from Whisper.

"You and Lukas are getting along great," Lauren said, beaming at the two of them. "And he's not easy to handle with. Remember Tommy riding him in the obstacle race? He did okay, though."

Jina nodded. She was glad Lauren had noticed how well Lukas was doing. "How could I forget?" she said. "They beat me and Three Bars Jake."

For a minute, they rode in silence. Jina gazed at the canopy of tall trees, their branches bare of leaves. They looked like old men and women with gnarled limbs. No wonder Lukas got jumpy whenever something rustled.

"Do you want to trot?" Lauren asked. "I want to catch up with the others and see how Andie's doing on Ranger. Her knee was pretty stiff this morning."

"No, you go on ahead. Lukas and I are happy plodding along." Just then, Lukas sidestepped nervously, and Jina laughed. "I guess he never really plods."

"Well, don't get too far behind or Katherine will have a fit," Lauren said. She started posting, as Whisper trotted briskly up the road. Lukas jumped forward, wanting to go with them. Jina used her seat and voice to steady him.

"No, you aren't following Whisper," Jina scolded him. "You just listen to me."

Reluctantly, the gelding settled into a bouncy walk. Jina smiled.

She and Lukas *were* doing okay.

So why couldn't she handle Applejacks?

Maybe Mrs. Caufield was right. Maybe she, Jina, had totally lost her confidence.

"I *am* a good rider," Jina said out loud, trying to convince herself. "I *can* ride tough horses like Lukas."

But all they were doing was poking along on the trail. What did that prove?

Suddenly, Lukas twirled toward a rotten stump. Head high, nostrils flaring, he snorted at a chipmunk scurrying into its hole.

Jina patted him reassuringly. "Hey, you're a hundred times bigger than that chipmunk. Quit being such a baby."

Lukas didn't seem completely convinced. He lowered his head and sniffed at the hole. Beside the stump, a narrow trail angled off the road, widening as it led into the forest. A small cross-country jump had been built across it.

Jina's heart began to thump excitedly. She

hadn't jumped since the day Superstar bowed his tendon.

Jina knew Lukas could jump. She'd watched Tommy guide him expertly around the obstacle course. She could get him over one small jump.

She could do it.

Closing her legs firmly against Lukas's sides, Jina steered him down the path. The jump, which was made of stacked logs, was about two feet high.

Lukas's ears flicked nervously. Jina collected him. As they neared the jump, she could feel his muscles tense. Using voice, seat, and reins, she urged him closer.

He reached the jump, hesitated, then leaped over it like a deer. Jina stayed with him easily. They landed and cantered down the path. They halted, turned, and cantered back over the fence. Lukas was smoother this time, like Pegasus, the mythical winged horse, flying through the clouds.

When they reached the logging road, Jina slowed the gelding to a walk.

"We did it!" she cried, flinging her arms around his neck.

I did it!

Jina grinned. Now she was ready to catch up with her friends. But not to tell them what she and Lukas had done.

The jump would be her secret.

"A bunch of us are going to the mall this afternoon," Andie told Jina at lunch. They were standing in the hot food line. "I need to buy some new underwear. Mine are shot."

Mary Beth peered around Jina's shoulder. "Well, if you'd wash them once in a while, maybe, they'd last longer," she said with a giggle.

Andie didn't even look up. "You're a loser, Finney. So are you coming with us?" she asked Jina.

"Well, I'd sure like to go to the mall," Jina said. She picked up a bowl of steaming vegetable soup. The taco salad smelled great, but she didn't think it would agree with her stomach. It was still feeling a little queasy.

"The minivan leaves at one-thirty," Andie said.

"Well, I really shouldn't go."

Andie looked at her curiously. "Why not?"

"Um." Jina hesitated, then mumbled, "I have to ride Applejacks."

Andie picked up her tray. "You have to ride *who?*" she asked loudly.

Jina glanced nervously around the lunchroom. "Shh!" she warned. Then she whispered, "Applejacks."

"Oh. So why the big secret?"

Jina picked up her own tray and followed Andie to the condiment table.

"It's no secret," she said. "It's just no big deal, okay?"

"Oh, I get it," Andie said as she squirted hot sauce all over her taco salad. "You just don't want us tagging along to Middlefield. You're afraid we'll steal Spencer from you."

Jina rolled her eyes. "Will you forget about Spencer? I'm not even going to Middlefield." Picking up her tray again, she followed Andie toward the table where Lauren was sitting. "Todd's bringing Applejacks to Foxhall."

Andie stopped in her tracks. "Uh-oh."

"What?"

"Tiffany. Over there, sitting next to Lauren. She keeps bugging us all about that stupid English project. That's one reason we're going to the mall."

Jina looked across the room. Tiffany was showing Lauren a copy of *Black Beauty*. Lauren was trying to listen and eat her salad at the same time.

Jina made a face. The thought of doing schoolwork with Tiffany on a Saturday made even riding Applejacks sound fun.

When she reached the table, she sat down next to Andie. Mary Beth arrived a few moments later. Saturday meals were usually informal, so the girls could sit anywhere and wear whatever they wanted—even their riding clothes.

When everyone was seated, Tiffany pulled a sheet of notebook paper from the book. "I'm getting really excited about this English project," she said. "Listen to what I've written so far. It's the beginning of our play."

Clearing her throat dramatically, she started to read:

"Joe: Oh, Beauty. Oh, Beauty. You are hot and tired! What should I do?

"Beauty: Don't give me that bucket of

water, Master. I want a rubdown and bran mash.

"Joe: Thank you, Beauty. You are such a smart horse! (He rubs Beauty with a towel.)

"Beauty: And thank *you*, Master. You are such a smart boy!"

With a proud grin, Tiffany looked around the table. "So what do you think?"

No one said anything. Jina knew she didn't want to be the first to tell Tiffany that her play stunk. And neither did anyone else.

Suddenly, Andie pushed her chair away from the table so she was behind Tiffany. Grabbing her own throat, she pretended to throw up.

Jina started laughing so hard, she choked on a spoonful of soup. Beside her, Lauren and Mary Beth snorted and gagged as they tried to muffle their laughter.

Just as quickly, Andie sat forward again, a serious expression on her face. "Gee, Tiffany, I like it a lot."

That made Mary Beth and Lauren crack up all over again. Tiffany's blue eyes turned icy.

Jina bit her lip and tried to wipe the smile off her face. She couldn't blame Tiffany for being mad.

"They're just teasing, Tiffany," she told the blond girl. "It's really good. Honest."

"Sure."

Tiffany stood up in a huff and grabbed her tray and book, then stalked over to another table.

"You went too far, Andie," Jina said, as Mary Beth and Lauren collapsed into giggles again.

"So?" Andie said. "At least I'm not teasing you about getting dumped off teeny-weeny Applejacks." Leaning across the table, she whispered loudly to Lauren and Mary Beth, "Jina's riding that fat pony right here at Foxhall this afternoon."

"Really?" Lauren turned to Jina. "That's great. How come?"

"Thanks, Andie," Jina grumbled.

"What? What did I do?" Andie looked around innocently. "You told me it wasn't a secret."

"It isn't. I just don't need an audience, okay?" Jina grabbed a cracker from her tray and snapped it in two.

"Don't worry, we're not going to watch," Mary Beth assured her. "We're going to the mall, right, guys?"

"Right." Lauren nodded seriously. "Andie needs new *underwear.*" Covering her mouth, she started to giggle again.

Jina closed her eyes and took a deep breath. Sometimes her roommates really drove her crazy.

They just wouldn't understand how important this afternoon was to her. She hadn't told her friends about Whitney's tantrum. She hadn't told them about the Chamberses not wanting her to ride Applejacks.

She hadn't told them that today was her very last chance with Applejacks.

After lunch, Jina trudged up the hill toward the Foxhall stables. Her helmet was tucked under her arm. Dark clouds hid the sun, and an icy wind whistled through the bare treetops.

Jina shivered. She was wearing her new winter riding coat that her mom had ordered from Jina's favorite riding catalog, so she should have been toasty warm. It was her nerves that were making her shake.

Jina had thought she'd gained her confidence back after her ride on Lukas. But now all that confidence seemed to have disappeared. What if Applejacks finally bucked her off?

"Jina! Wait up!"

Jina turned to see who was calling to her.

Mary Beth, Lauren, and Andie were hurrying up the hill behind her, dressed in cold-weather gear.

Jina groaned. Her roommates hadn't gone to the Woodville mall as they'd planned. They were coming to watch her.

"Why aren't you guys at the mall?" Jina asked when her roommates caught up with her. She tried not to sound too annoyed.

"Well, just before the minivan loaded up, we decided the mall sounded *boring* compared to watching Rotten Apple run off with you," Andie said with a grin. A striped cap was tilted rakishly over her bushy hair.

"That's not true," Lauren objected. She wore a blue Polarfleece cap, a bright red ski jacket, and fur-lined boots. "We decided you needed us more. To cheer you on."

Mary Beth nodded in agreement. Her mother had sent her a hand-knitted scarf that was about seven feet long. It hung all the way to her knees.

"That's right," she said. "*We* know you're a great rider, even if Applejacks dumps you."

"Gee, thanks, guys," Jina said through her teeth. She knew her roommates were trying to be nice, but why couldn't everyone just leave her alone for once?

"I didn't have any money to spend, anyway," Mary Beth added gloomily as they went up the hill together.

Jina stopped in the stable courtyard. The Middlefield horse van was pulling up the drive. Mrs. Caufield and Katherine Parks, came out of the office. Then Jina noticed a car behind the van.

Her heart sunk. It was the Chamberses' Mercedes!

Mr. Chambers was driving. Whitney sat in the passenger seat. When she saw the girls, she bounced up and down excitedly.

"Boy, the whole world's going to be watching you, Jina," Mary Beth said.

"Thanks for pointing that out, Mary Beth," Jina said. "I feel a lot less nervous now."

When the Mercedes stopped, Whitney jumped out. She rushed straight to Jina and gave her a hug. "This is going to be so much fun!" the little girl exclaimed. "I love Foxhall. How's Superstar? Can I see him later? Will you let me sit on him bareback?" Jina's eyes widened. She couldn't believe Whitney was being so friendly. Had she forgotten all about her temper tantrum on Wednesday and how she didn't want her riding Applejacks anymore?

Before Jina could reply, Whitney darted over to Lauren and Mary Beth. Grabbing their hands, she pulled them toward the horse van. "Come on," she said, tugging hard. "Let's go watch Todd unload Apple."

Jina walked slowly to the tack room. For a moment, she rested her forehead against the flap of her schooling saddle, willing herself to be calm. She had composed herself for dozens of major shows. This shouldn't be any different. Why was this little pony upsetting her so much?

Half an hour later, Jina was mounted on Applejacks. They stood in the middle of the indoor arena. Mrs. Caufield walked around them, studying Jina's position.

Applejack's ears were tilted back. Jina could tell by his sour expression that he didn't like her any better at Foxhall.

Whitney, Mary Beth, Lauren, and Andie huddled in a corner. Since Foxhall's indoor arena wasn't as fancy as Middlefield's, there was no place to sit.

Jina could tell the girls were trying to be quiet, but every so often she heard a burst of muffled giggling.

Todd, Katherine, and Mr. Chambers stood in the arena entrance. Jina had never met Mr. Chambers before. He was short with a trim mustache. His arms were folded in front of his chest as he watched Jina, a stern look on his face.

She sighed, feeling completely discouraged.

Mrs. Caufield chuckled. "Don't give up already, Jina. This pony does look awfully sour, though." Puzzled, she shook her head. "I can't imagine why. You're sitting on him nicely."

She glanced up at Jina again. "Okay, let's see him go. And don't forget. If he tries to buck, sit deep, grab his mane with your left hand, and jerk his head up and around with your right rein."

With a nod, Jina squeezed her legs against Applejacks's sides. The pony flattened his ears as he started across the arena.

"Try voice commands only," Mrs. Caufield suggested. "He may not be used to leg aids."

Jina totally relaxed her legs. Applejacks's stride seemed to smooth out a little. She circled him in front of her roommates and Whitney. The younger girl was babbling away, trying to get the others' attention.

"That's good!" Mrs. Caufield called. "Go ahead and trot. Keep your legs super-quiet." Jina trotted Applejacks twice around the arena. The second time around, his ears finally pricked up and he gazed curiously at his surroundings.

Jina began to breathe easier.

"Halt."

She barely closed her fingers around the pony's reins and he immediately put on the brakes.

Mrs. Caufield approached, a smile on her face. "I think we may have found the problem. You might be too *good* a rider for Applejacks, Miss Williams. Perhaps your aids have been too direct and forceful. This pony is used to receiving voice commands when Todd longes him. And Whitney's legs are too short to be very effective."

Jina smiled faintly. "I hope that's the problem."

"Try cantering him. Ride him the same way—as if you're just a passenger. Don't throw his head entirely away, of course," she added.

Jina steered the pony to the outside of the

arena. She sat deep, then touched him with her outside heel. At the same time, she told him to canter.

Applejacks broke into a smooth canter. Jina grinned happily and began to relax. Suddenly, without warning, the pony ducked his head, pulling the reins between her fingers.

With stiff legs, he crow-hopped across the arena. Jina's feet flew from the stirrups, and she landed hard in the saddle.

Before she could even grab mane, Applejacks rounded his back and bucked high in the air. The violent movement tossed Jina skyward.

With a startled cry, she hurtled toward the ground.

"Jina! Are you okay?" Whitney was the first person to rush over.

Jina winced. She'd fallen on her shoulder, and it definitely hurt. Luckily, the tanbark in the arena was deep, so the injury probably wasn't serious.

Slowly, she sat up. Mrs. Caufield hurried over and stooped down next to her. Jina looked around for Applejacks. Tail high, head arched, the pony was prancing around the far end of the arena. Todd was walking slowly toward him, his hand outstretched.

"Are you all right?" Mrs. Caufield asked worriedly.

Jina brushed her dirty hands off on her thighs. She was too embarrassed to meet Mrs. Caufield's eyes.

When she finally glanced up, Whitney was staring at her. The little girl had a strange look on her face. Jina couldn't tell if she was concerned—or happy.

"Yeah, I'm fine." Rising to her feet, Jina swiped at the tanbark clinging to her breeches. "Sorry. Apple bucked so fast I couldn't stop him."

Mrs. Caufield didn't say anything. Jina could feel her roommates' eyes boring into her back. She could also hear Mr. Chambers talking to Todd in a low voice.

Her whole body went rigid. She felt as if she couldn't breathe. In all her life she'd never felt like such a failure.

"Really, I'm fine," she repeated, though no one had said a thing. She turned her gaze to Whitney. The little girl was biting her lip.

"You've got your wish, Whitney," Jina said, feeling strangely calm. "I won't ever ride Applejacks again."

I'm not going to think about it. I'm not going to cry, Jina told herself a few minutes later. *It's over.*

She was in Superstar's stall. Her fingers were twined in the Thoroughbred's mane, her face buried in his warm neck. As he munched the last of his breakfast hay, he turned his head to look at her.

Jina squeezed her eyelids shut so tightly she started to see bright colors.

"I really am okay," she said out loud, hoping to convince herself. She just didn't want to see or talk to anyone for the rest of her life.

Breathing raggedly, her shoulder still aching, Jina turned and reached around the doorjamb for the grooming kit she'd left in the aisle. A sudden rustling noise made her jerk her hand back with a start.

A mouse? she wondered.

Slowly, she poked her head into the aisle. Whitney was sitting next to the grooming kit, her head resting on her bent knees. Her arms covered the sides of her face. Quiet sobs shook her body.

Jina frowned. "Whitney? What are you doing here?" She slid the stall door open wider, then shut it behind her as she stepped into the aisle. She kneeled down next to the little girl.

Whitney's sobs grew louder.

Jina studied her suspiciously. Was she really upset about something, or was this dramatic scene just another one of her games?

Sitting back on her heels, Jina let the little girl cry. After a few minutes, her sobs turned to gasps, then hiccups.

Finally, Whitney glanced up. Her eyes were puffy and red. *If she is faking, she's doing a great job*, Jina thought.

"Want to tell me about it?" Jina asked.

Whitney shook her head no. Then she suddenly changed her mind and nodded yes.

Jina waited.

"I—I—don't want you to stop riding Applejacks," the little girl said.

Surprised, Jina said, "Why not? All he does is buck me off."

Whitney's lower lip trembled. Her eyes glistened with tears. "He doesn't mean to!" she blurted. "He really likes you. He told me he'd miss you if you went away. He says—he says—" She hiccuped. "He says you're his only friend "

Jina's heart softened. "Oh-h-h-h." She nodded. "I see." And she did see. Obviously, Applejacks wasn't going to miss her. But it was the only way Whitney knew to tell Jina that *she* would.

Jina covered Whitney's hand with hers. "And I'll miss Applejacks, too. But you know who I'll really miss?"

"Who?" Whitney squeaked.

"You."

"Oh, Jina!" Falling into Jina's lap, the little girl started crying all over again. Jina stroked her curly hair, wondering why she was so miserable.

"I'm sorry I said you weren't my friend anymore," Whitney whispered. "I didn't mean it."

"That's okay. You were mad."

Whitney's head popped up. "I'm mad at everybody!" she cried. "Especially my mommy and daddy!"

Jina's brows shot up. "Why?"

"Because—because, they yell at each other all the time. And they're getting a divorce." Angrily, Whitney swiped at the tears running down her cheeks. "I hate them."

Jina didn't know what to say. She thought back to all of Whitney's tantrums and spoiled, demanding behavior. Was the little girl acting that way because she was angry and confused about her parents' divorce?

Maybe. *And maybe if I hadn't been so wrapped up in my own problems with Applejacks, I would have realized something was wrong*, Jina told herself.

"Parents don't think sometimes," Jina said

finally. "They don't always realize how much they hurt their children."

She thought about her own mom. Myra Golden was beautiful, famous, charming, generous, and loving. But she was also superbusy with her TV show. So busy she didn't have much time left for Jina.

Jina sighed. "I'm sorry you didn't tell me sooner. Maybe I could have helped."

Sniffing loudly, Whitney sat up. "Can you sleep over at my house sometime?" she asked, a hopeful look in her blue eyes.

Jina smiled. "Maybe."

"How about tonight?"

Jina laughed. "Not tonight. I have to get special permission from the office ahead of time. It's kind of a big deal to spend the night off campus."

"Oh." Whitney's face fell.

Jina leaned over and hugged her. "But we'll do it soon. And even if I don't ride Applejacks anymore, we can still be friends."

"Whitney!" someone called sharply. Mr. Chambers poked his head through the partly open doorway. "We have to go."

Whitney scrambled to her feet. "I'm coming," she said quickly.

But over her shoulder, she flashed Jina a shy smile. Jina gave her the thumbs-up sign.

Whitney's father grabbed her hand and steered her from the barn. Jina wondered if he had any idea how unhappy his daughter was. Probably not.

Jina leaned her head back against the wall. She was glad she'd patched things up with Whitney. Maybe she'd even be able to help her little friend get through a hard time.

And what about your problem with Applejacks? Jina thought to herself. Well, that was solved, too. She would never ride him again—ever.

Just then Superstar stuck his head over the Dutch door. Hay fell from between his rubbery lips. He snuffled Jina's hair as if trying to make her feel better. She reached up to stroke his nose, but a sudden scraping noise made him snap his head up.

Lauren was sliding the barn door all the way open. Mary Beth followed behind her, carrying Jina's saddle. Seconds later, Andie hobbled down the aisle, too.

"We brought you your saddle," Lauren said, stopping in front of Jina.

Jina braced herself. She was ready for Lauren's pitying looks, Mary Beth's disappointment, and Andie's teasing.

"Yup." Andie swatted Superstar's neck. "We figured you were through riding Applejacks for today."

Mary Beth set the saddle against the wall. "Boy, I've never seen anyone get bucked off before! It was like watching a rodeo."

"Mary Beth!" Lauren warned.

Mary Beth flushed. "I mean, I'm glad you're all right, Jina. You know that."

"I know." Slowly, Jina stood up. "So what happened to Applejacks? Did Todd catch him?"

Her three roommates glanced at one another, pained expressions on their faces. Mary Beth pulled on her bangs, and Lauren chewed on her lower lip. Even Andie wouldn't meet Jina's eyes.

Jina frowned at them. "What's wrong? Was Applejacks hurt?"

Lauren shook her head. "No. But Todd sure was mad at him!" Her gaze darted toward Andie and Mary Beth.

Jina plunked her fists on her hips. "Will you guys tell me what's wrong? I can handle it. It can't be any worse than getting bucked off in front of everybody."

"That's what you think," Mary Beth mumbled.

Andie threw up her hands. "Come on, guys. We might as well tell her. She's going to find out anyway."

"Find out what?"

Andie faced Jina. "After you left, Todd caught Applejacks and took off your saddle. Then Mrs. Caufield asked Katherine to get on him—she's light enough—and Todd said okay."

"So Katherine got her own saddle," Mary Beth chimed in, "and got on Apple. And..." Her voice trailed off.

"And?" Jina prompted.

"And he went *perfectly*," Andie said. "Katherine even jumped him. Then when we were leaving, we overheard Todd and Mrs. Caufield talking. They said—" Andie hesitated.

Jina raised her eyebrows. "They said what? I can take it."

"They said there was nothing wrong with Applejacks," Andie finished in a rush. "And you were definitely the problem, Jina!"

Jina stared blankly at her roommates, trying to look as if she didn't care what Mrs. Caufield and Todd had said about her. Even though it was the truth. Even though it hurt.

"Well," Jina said finally trying to sound cheerful, "that's no big surprise. Whitney and Katherine can ride Applejacks. I can't." She shrugged. "It doesn't take a genius to figure out that I'm the problem."

Turning abruptly, she grabbed the handle of her grooming kit and, pushing past Andie, jerked open the stall door, marched inside, and dropped the kit on the floor.

Superstar snorted and backed out of her way. "I'm not mad at you, you big dummy," Jina muttered. Ignoring her roommates, she started to curry him.

Maybe they'll go away, she thought.

The barn was silent for a few minutes. Jina wondered if her friends had finally gotten the hint and left. She peeked over her shoulder. Lauren was hanging over the top of the Dutch door, watching her.

Jina rolled her eyes. Lauren could be pretty dense about hints.

When Lauren didn't say anything for what seemed like forever, Jina finally asked, "Where did Mary Beth and Andie go?"

"Andie's walking Magic and Mary Beth went to groom Dan."

So why don't you leave, too? Jina wanted to ask. She just curried harder.

"Uh, there's one more thing," Lauren said.

"What?" Jina asked, gritting her teeth.

"Todd is leaving Applejacks here until tomorrow. Mrs. Caufield wants Katherine to ride him one more time, just to make sure he's safe."

"That's nice." Jina knew she sounded rude, but she didn't care.

Lauren cleared her throat. "You know, Jina, I still think you're the best rider at Foxhall. If you ask me, there's got to be a good reason why Applejacks acts so funny when you ride him."

Jina stopped currying, and her shoulders drooped. "Yeah, well, thanks, Lauren. But if there is a reason, I sure don't know what it is."

Lauren nodded. "Well, I'll see you later," she said. She sounded just as down as Jina.

"See you," Jina said.

As soon as Lauren had left, Jina sagged against Superstar's neck.

All her fears had come true. She hadn't been able to ride Applejacks, and now everyone—except for maybe Lauren—thought she was a lousy rider.

Jina picked up a dandy brush and furiously stroked it along Superstar's side.

Her heart felt hollow. She knew she shouldn't care what everybody thought. But she couldn't help it. And it wasn't just the whole disaster with Applejacks. Ever since she'd arrived at Foxhall, she'd wanted to fit in and be liked. But somehow everything always seemed to go wrong.

With a sigh, Jina tossed the brush into the bucket. Snapping a lead to Superstar's halter, she led him out the stall door. She wanted to take him behind the barn and let him eat some of the still-green grass.

When they stepped outside, the sun was peeking through the clouds. Jina led Superstar to a protected corner in front of the paddocks. Immediately, he dropped his head and hungrily snatched at the grass.

Jina leaned against his warm, fuzzy side. Another horse was grazing in one of the paddocks. *Not a horse*, Jina corrected herself, *a pony*. Then she realized the pony was Applejacks.

Mrs. Caufield must have told Todd to leave him back there. Jina squinted her eyes, staring at him. He looked so cute and innocent, his thick pony forelock hanging between his ears like bangs.

Jina thought back to what Lauren had said: "*I still think you're the best rider at Foxhall.*" And Mrs. Caufield had enough confidence in her to assign her Lukas for the trail ride.

So why can't I ride Applejacks? Jina asked herself for the hundredth time. It didn't made sense. It couldn't be all her fault.

What else could it be?

Superstar moved closer to the paddock, pulling Jina with him. He cropped the grass around the fence posts, one eye watching Applejacks.

Curious, the pony ambled over and stuck his head over the fence. Jina rubbed him behind the ears. When she stopped, he nudged her with his nose, begging for more.

"So why are you so friendly now?" she asked. "Is it because I'm not going to ride you? Is it because I'm not holding a saddle, ready to tack you up?"

The saddle!

Jina froze. Why hadn't she thought about that before? Her mind began to race as she remembered an article she'd read about problem horses.

Wearing a saddle is like wearing shoes, the article had said. *If the fit's not exactly right, the result is misery for the horse.*

Had Applejacks been miserable in her saddle? Was that why he'd given her nasty looks whenever she'd saddled him? Was that why he'd hollowed his back whenever Jina rode him?

Whitney and Katherine had used different saddles.

Superstar was twice as big as Apple. Maybe his saddles had fit the pony all wrong.

Maybe, just maybe, the problem isn't me! Jina thought excitedly.

She had to find out for sure. She had to ride Applejacks—bareback.

"Come here, Superstar." Jina tugged his head out of the grass. "I'm putting you in the other paddock for a minute. You can eat there."

Jina latched the gate, then ran into the barn and grabbed her helmet from on top of her grooming kit. When she raced outside, Applejacks was still hanging over the fence, watching Superstar.

As she neared the paddock gate, Jina hesitated. She knew she shouldn't get on him alone. Should she go tell Mrs. Caufield her idea about the saddle?

No, she decided quickly. If the riding director was convinced that Jina was the problem, she would only think Jina was making excuses.

She had to do this on her own.

With new determination, Jina opened the gate. Her arm outstretched as if she had a treat, she carefully approached Applejacks. When he sniffed at her hand, she hooked the lead onto the left side of his halter. Then she looped it over his neck and tied the end to the right side of the halter like reins.

Jina took a deep breath. Her burst of confidence was waning. If her idea about the saddle was wrong, Applejacks would probably throw her a mile.

But she had to take that chance.

Without hesitation, Jina mounted him. Jumping up and across his back, she pulled herself over. Applejacks stood quietly.

She gathered the rope reins. Her heart was pounding so hard she could feel it in her chest. Applejacks had to know she was scared stiff.

"Walk." The pony strode off, his stride long and flowing. Jina steered him around the paddock. She watched, waiting for his usual pinned-back ears and nasty looks. But his ears were pricked forward, his gaze curious.

Feeling encouraged, Jina clucked and squeezed lightly with her legs, which were hanging long against his sides. He broke into an easy trot. Jina bounced on his back.

For a second, she tensed, ready for his hollow-backed, jolting crow hops. But they never came.

Smoothly and willingly, the pony trotted around the paddock. Jina couldn't believe it.

Everybody had been wrong, including her. *She* wasn't the problem. It was definitely the saddle!

A blur of color and movement caught Jina's eye. She halted Applejacks.

Andie, Lauren, and Mary Beth were coming around the corner of the barn. When they saw Jina on Applejacks, the three of them stopped dead in their tracks.

Lauren was the first to rush over to the paddock fence. "What are you doing?" she gasped.

Jina walked Applejacks to the gate. "I did it!" she said, beaming. "I did it!" Lying on the pony's neck, she wrapped her arms around him.

"You rode him *bareback?*" Andie asked, her eyes wide with amazement. "After he bucked you off?"

Jina nodded, her cheek still pressed in the pony's wiry mane. "Yes. And he was perfect. It wasn't *me*. It wasn't *me* he hated!"

Her roommates just stared at her, confused.

"Then what was it?" Mary Beth asked.

"My saddles!" Jina said.

"The saddles?" the three exclaimed in unison.

"Are you sure?" Lauren asked.

Jina told them about the magazine article, and how the other people who had ridden Apple had used their own saddles.

"So my saddles had to be the only things that were different," Jina explained excitedly. "I should have guessed when he pinned his ears back every time I went to saddle him. I only wish I'd found out sooner. Poor Applejacks must have been so uncomfortable!"

Andie shook her head. "Wow," was all she said.

"What are you guys doing here, anyway?" Jina asked.

"We thought you might need some cheering up," Lauren said.

Andie snickered. "Yeah, we still like you, even if you did get dumped."

"Besides, Tiffany was hanging around the suite wanting to work on that dumb English project," Mary Beth added.

Jina gathered her rope reins. "I'm going to canter him," she declared.

Mary Beth's mouth dropped. "Jina! Don't

do that. I don't want to see you get bucked off again."

Jina straightened. "I'm not going to get bucked off, Mary Beth. Everything's going to be okay. Cantering will prove it."

Mary Beth frowned, looking unconvinced. Even Andie and Lauren looked at each other with worried expressions.

"Don't try and talk me out of it," Jina said firmly as she steered Applejacks away from the fence. Her own heart was racing. She didn't need to see the doubt in her roommates' eyes. She was going to prove once and for all that she wasn't a lousy rider.

Before she could chicken out, Jina gave Applejacks the signal to canter. Smooth as silk, the pony loped around the paddock.

Lauren, Andie, and Mary Beth clapped and cheered.

A sob of happiness caught in Jina's throat. If only she'd figured out the saddle thing earlier, Applejacks wouldn't have been so miserable.

She wouldn't have been so miserable.

But then maybe she wouldn't have found out about Whitney's being miserable. And maybe she wouldn't have worked so hard to solve her own problem.

Grinning proudly, Jina halted Applejacks in front of her roommates.

"Not bad, Williams," Andie said. "You two just might be ready for next Saturday's show."

"We just might." Jina couldn't stop smiling.

Lauren peered up at her. "Didn't I say you were the best rider at Foxhall?"

Jina nodded. "You did. I don't think I'm the best," she added quickly.

"Come on, Williams. Even I have to admit you're pretty good," Andie said. "The whole time Rotten Apple was bucking you off, I knew it wasn't really your fault."

"It's too bad it took *you* so long to believe it!" Lauren added.

"Yeah, too bad," Jina agreed. Sliding off Applejacks, she gave him another big hug.

Don't miss the next book in the Riding Academy series: #8: THE CRAZIEST HORSE SHOW EVER

"The vans are here!" Jina called.

Andie and Lauren ran eagerly to the trailer that held Ranger and Whisper, just as Katherine Parks climbed down from the truck.

"What's wrong?" Lauren asked.

Katherine frowned. "Ranger stomped and kicked the whole ride."

"Is he okay?" Andie asked anxiously. Without waiting for an answer, she swung open the trailer's front door and stuck her head inside.

Ranger kicked and pawed the rubber mat. His neck was dark with sweat.

"Let's unload him," Katherine said as she unlatched the trailer ramp.

Andie hooked the lead rope onto Ranger's halter and unsnapped him from the quick release trailer tie. "Ready!" she called back.

Lauren ran around to help Katherine. When the two of them lowered the heavy tailgate to the ground, Lauren gasped.

It was splashed with blood!

ALISON HART has been horse crazy since she was five years old. Her first pony was a pinto named Ted.

"I rode Ted bareback because we didn't have a saddle small enough," she says.

Now Ms. Hart lives and writes in Mt. Sidney, Virginia, with her husband, two kids, two dogs, one cat, her horse, April, and another pinto pony named Marble. A former teacher, she spends much of her time visiting schools to talk to her many Riding Academy fans. And you guessed it—she's still horse crazy!